Goddess for Hire

GODDESS FOR HIRE

Sonia Singh

AVON
TRADE

An Imprint of HarperCollinsPublishers

HarperCollins books may be purchased for education, business, or sales promotional use. For information please write: Special Markets Department, HarperCollins Publishers Inc., 10 East 53rd Street, New York, NY 10022.

FIRST EDITION

Designed by Elizabeth M. Glover

Library of Congress Cataloging-in-Publication Data

Singh, Sonia.
   Goddess for hire / Sonia Singh.—1st ed.
      p. cm.
ISBN 0-06-059036-X
1. East Indian American women—Fiction. 2. Orange County (Calif.)—Fiction.
3. Kālā (Hindu deity)—Fiction. 4. Young women—Fiction.
5. Goddesses—Fiction. I. Title.

PS3619.I5745G63   2004
813'.6—dc22   2003063937

04 05 06 07 08 JTC/RRD 10 9 8 7 6 5 4 3 2

This book is dedicated to my mother, Manjeet, who agreed to pay for all my writing classes if I promised not to get drunk and dance on the tables at any more Indian gatherings.

Okay, so I've yet to keep my end of the bargain . . .

Seriously, Mom—

Thank you!

And no, I didn't forget you guys—

My dad, Bob; my brother, Samir (who, even as a zygote, showed far more sense than six-year-old me); my sister, Anita; Max; and my grandfather, Gurdial Singh Sindhi, who taught me to cherish books and always keep them close.

Acknowledgments

Many thanks to two of my favorite New Yorkers:

Kimberly Whalen—my dream agent, who not only has super powers, but believed in *Goddess* from the start and encouraged me to call whenever I felt anxious and insecure.

By the way, Kim, you've yet to give me your new phone number . . .

Lyssa Keusch—my brilliant and generous editor, whose creative insights are so enlightened that all across India, meditating swamis whisper her name in hushed reverence.

My thanks wouldn't be complete without a decibel-shattering shout-out to Kim and Lyssa's fab assistants—Rebecca Strauss and May Chen.

My crew: Nakul Mahajan, Simi Singh, Rebeca Ladron de Guevara, Amit Singh, Michael Cochran, Lucinda Ferguson, Shelly de Simone, and Gary Mecija.

My writing teachers: Sean Hulbert, Terry Black, and Louella Nelson.

Acknowledgments

And no, I didn't forget you guys either—

My extended family: Romel Bhullar, Maya Lalvani, the Mahajans, the Saggars, the Brars, the "other" Singhs, the Ahujas, the Jollys, the Hotanis, the Lalvanis, and Aruna Chandiramani.

GODDESS FOR HIRE

Chapter 1

I NEVER BELIEVED in dharma, karma, reincarnation, or any of that spiritual crap, which caused sort of a problem growing up because my parents are devout Hindus. Dharma, by the way, means life purpose in Sanskrit. By the time my thirtieth birthday rolled around, I still hadn't found my dharma, which caused my parents some worry, [read: anxiety, loss of sleep, despair, hand-wringing, tears, dizzy spells and a constant mumbling of nasty things about me in Hindi under their breath].

My birthday fell on the second Saturday of January, and as I zipped down Pacific Coast Highway in my canary yellow Hummer H2, I thought about upgrading to a bigger car.

Newport Beach, where we live, is a nice-looking beach city. Streets are wide, cars are expensive, bodies are beautiful, and neighborhoods are well tended. A French Colonial–style roof is not allowed when the zoning laws call for Spanish. For your coffee-drinking pleasure there is a Starbucks on every corner.

I like living in a place where the air is clean and neighbors hide their trash in discreet garbage cans made to blend in with the shrubbery. I am, however, tired of the impression that blond, blue-eyed families are the sole inhabitants of Newport Beach. This isn't Sweden for God's sake.

Indian people like to bitch about the big bad British ruling India for two hundred years. Big deal. Try growing up in Orange County. Most of my cousins sport blue contact lenses and dye their hair ash-blond. How's that for colonial impact?

For the record, I do not dye my dark tresses. I do, however, highlight.

I'd spent the afternoon enjoying a manicure and pedicure at the Bella Salon and Spa, followed by shopping at South Coast Plaza. My birthday happened to fall on a Saturday, but even if it hadn't, my plan would have been the same, one of the benefits to being unemployed.

Eight shopping bags later I was back in my SUV slurping on a Mocha Frappuccino. I'm not into meditation, and I don't do yoga. I don't blast sitar music in my car either. I prefer Madonna. I turned up the volume and felt my spirits rise.

As if it hadn't been bad enough rolling out of bed this morning knowing it was the start of my third decade, the night before my aunt Gayatri, a gynecologist, had come over to the house lugging an enormous chart of the female reproductive system.

By the time she was done I knew more about my

vulva than I ever wanted to, and that I was fast on my way to acquiring the shriveled ovaries of a crone. Basically my dear aunt was hinting I'd better find a man and reproduce then and there. Well duh! She couldn't have been less subtle if she'd hit me over the head with the pink plastic vagina she kept in the car.

In traditional Indian culture, a woman is supposed to get married and have children—strictly in that order—by the time she's twenty-five. My female cousins and I, having been born and raised in America, have it considerably harder, not easier. We're all supposed to get married, have children, and be either a doctor, lawyer, or engineer, all by the time we're twenty-five.

My female cousins all found proper careers, married proper Indian boys, had proper Indian weddings, and properly lavish wedding receptions. If I ever get married, I definitely will not have some decrepit Hindu priest muttering in Sanskrit while pouring clarified butter over a fire, as I struggle not to inhale great quantities of smoke, praying frantically that my sari doesn't unravel, fall off, or burst into flames.

Now instead of spending my birthday with people whose company I enjoyed, I was on my way home to have dinner with my family. The last thing I wanted to do was eat Indian food and discuss recent advances in medical science. Hobnobbing with doctors wasn't my idea of fun. If it were, I'd be crashing AMA conferences across the state.

My mom's a pediatrician in private practice, my dad, a

renowned urologist, and I mean the man gets absolutely giddy over bladder infections. My younger brother, Samir, is in his final year at Stanford Medical School. In fact, of all the ninety-seven adult members of the Mehra clan spread throughout the United States, ninety-six are doctors, the sole exception being yours truly.

Thereby proving, that contrary to popular belief India produces far more doctors than snake charmers. I would put engineers at a close second and, okay, maybe snake charmers at third.

Thereby also proving, that if life were a vegetarian Indian buffet, I'd be one, big, steaming plate of haggis.

I thought fleetingly of avoiding the dinner tonight, but with my mom it wasn't a request, it was an order. God, just because I live at home and spend their money, my parents think they can tell me what to do.

Maybe it was the fact I was consuming a beverage, conversing on my cell phone, and steering my behemoth of a car, but I failed to notice the dark blue Mercedes S600 parked on the curb in front of our Mediterranean-style house. I pulled into the three-car garage, left the bags in the back for later, and stepped inside.

"Maya!" I was nearly knocked over as my aunt barreled into me. Now I'm not that tall, about five-three. Aunt Dimple, a dermatologist, barely comes up to my chin. In a detail that greatly puzzled me as a child, Aunt Dimple did not have a single dimple on her face. "Happy birthday! I can't wait to tell you my surprise!" As I stared down at her, I felt a sick malignant tumor of dread take form in my stomach.

"Tell her the news, Dimpy," my dad smiled.

The Queen of Retin-A, who cleared up my adolescent outbreak of acne, and was responsible for the glowing complexion I possess today, now stood in front of me, and I wanted nothing more than for the Earth to open up and swallow her plump, perky form.

It's hard to find an Indian family without an aunt Dimple. Aunt Dimples have one hobby and one hobby only.

Matchmaking.

At that moment, pink plastic vagina or not, I'd have given anything for my aunt Gayatri.

Chapter 2

"OH, I CAN'T WAIT to tell you!" My undimpled aunt gazed up at me beaming. "I've found you a boy."

I felt hysterical laughter bubbling up inside me. "A boy? Do I look like a Catholic priest?" I giggled.

No one joined in.

Aunt Dimple grabbed my hand and pulled me over to the sofa. "His name is Tahir, he's thirty-one and comes from one of the best families in Delhi."

"Why do they always come from the best families?" I pointed out. "Do the worst families have trouble hooking up? Do Indian parents ever come home to their kid and say, we found you someone from one of the worst families, there's insanity on the mother's side and inbreeding on the father's."

The silence was deafening.

My mom sat down on the other side, effectively barricading me in a matrimonial-minded sandwich. My dad plopped down in the recliner and turned on the *Nightly Business Report*, his parental duties done for the day.

I grabbed an embroidered sofa cushion and thought about smothering myself, but with three doctors in the room I'd be resuscitated before you could say "Om."

Now it's not as though I'm vehemently opposed to testosterone; like every other heterosexual single woman straddling thirty I was on the lookout for a man, and I wasn't asking for much. Just a man who respected me, fucked like a stallion, and still paid for dinner.

Not some Indian guy who saw me as his fast track to a green card.

Most Indian parents are Amish-strict about dating, but in a hurry to get you married. My mom didn't let me date until I was seventeen. My aunt Gayatri, the gynecologist, was even stricter. However that didn't stop her from happily discussing masturbation at the dinner table, and the best sexual positions for conceiving a son.

Aunt Dimple pulled a large manila envelope from her bag. "I have his picture and his bio data."

"Hey, why don't we put our heads together and find a cure for poverty in India?" I volunteered. "Now would be a great time—"

"I know I had his picture," Aunt Dimple interrupted, frowning into her bag.

"Just give her his bio data," my mom said. I glared at her. She stared back at me without blinking.

I grabbed the single sheet of paper from my aunt. "What, only one page?" I said sarcastically. Tahir's bio data listed his height, weight, education, ancestry, and favorite food . . . Chinese. "But what kind of person is he?"

8

"He's a nice boy," Aunt Dimple said. "I haven't actually met him, but his mother and I lunched at McDonald's. She's a very nice lady. We ate the most delicious Maharajah Macs. I think McDonald's tastes better in India, don't you? It's a status thing there, not like here."

Oh God, an Indian mother-in-law! I recalled the number of bride burnings in India where mothers-in-law shoved their new daughters-in-law into the oven after dutifully collecting their dowries. Would I find myself roasting nicely at 365 degrees?

I smiled with artificial brightness and started to rise. "I'm not interested, but thanks for thinking of me—"

"It's time you became an adult, Maya," my mom interrupted sternly. "When I was your age I was married, I had a child, and I was doing my residency at UCLA. You need some direction in your life."

"And marriage will give me that? Seriously, Mom, we're not living in the 1950s."

"In the 1950s you would've been a grandmother at your age," my aunt jumped in.

There was no point arguing with them. I slumped back against the sofa. Maybe Tahir would find me unmarriageable?

I quickly discarded that thought. I was gorgeous, possessed superb taste, and could make conversation at any cocktail party.

Really, there was only one solution to my problem.

I smiled and sat up. "So when do Tahir and I meet?"

My mom stared at me suspiciously, but my aunt relaxed and returned the smile. "His flight will be arriving tomorrow evening at LAX. I thought maybe the next day he could come for dinner?"

"Why don't I go and pick him up? It'll give us a chance to talk," I proposed innocently.

"Excellent." Aunt Dimple patted my cheek. "I know the two of you will hit it off. And I did have an extensive wart removal scheduled with a regular patient, so I was cutting it close. I would have asked your uncle, but he's performing an operation on this enormous hernia. Apparently it resembles Mickey Mouse's head and . . ."

I tuned out as my mom and aunt chatted on about the adventures of my uncle Pradeep, the proctologist.

Tomorrow morning I'd pick up Mr. Tahir at the airport and tell him, in no uncertain terms, he could get right back on the plane to Delhi.

Chapter 3

HIS FLIGHT was late.

I'd been stuck at LAX for over two hours. I toyed with the idea of going home, but the opportunity to talk to Tahir without my family as audience was too important to pass up. If need be, I'd spend the night curled up on one of the less than ergonomic airport seats.

I didn't have to perform such a sacrifice though; the flight finally arrived just three hours behind schedule. That's what happens when you fly Air India. Well that and spending twenty-three hours in a cabin that smells like curry. I prefer Lufthansa, efficient, clean, and they hand out Toblerone chocolates.

I lazily held out the small sign inscribed with Tahir's name, since I had no clue what he looked like, and waited with a flock of people as passengers passed wearily out of customs.

Personally I wouldn't set foot in India without a suitcase filled with antibacterial lotion. Last year my family went, along with our neighbors, the Marshalls. Why so many white people insist on dipping their toes in the Ganges is beyond me. So what if a dunk in the river erases all your bad karma? Dead people are cremated there. The Indian government had to introduce a breed of scavenger turtle in the water to dispose of rotting flesh.

Doesn't that just make you want to gag?

I made eye contact with various men of Indian origin, but other than the usual appraising male stares and come-hither smiles, none of them stopped, pointed at the sign, and said, "Namaste. I'm your future husband."

"You spelled my last name wrong," a clipped, precise, male voice said from my right. I turned and felt a rush of undiluted, uninhibited, God-bless-your-DNA, animal lust.

He was tall, six feet or so, with thick, wavy black hair, flashing black eyes fringed by long lashes, a soft, sensuous mouth, fabulous skin the shade of dark honey, and the type of body that would make half of Hollywood's top males run crying to their personal trainers.

"Tahir?" I gasped.

"My last name is spelled S-A-H-N-I."

"Huh?" I looked down to where I'd written, "Tahir Sawney" on the sign. "How was your flight?" I managed to articulate.

"Beastly," he said curtly. "Business class has absolutely gone to the dogs. Some bloody passengers caused a fuss demanding buffalo milk, and behind me this swami continually rang and rang for the attendant. After the meal the fool burned a stick of incense in the lavatory, setting off the fire alarm. We nearly had to emergency land in Osaka."

"Well you must be exhausted, my car isn't too far—"

"Let me clear up a little matter first," Tahir interrupted. He gazed intently into my eyes. "I have no intention of marrying you. I have hordes of desperate, socially acceptable women chasing me in Delhi, which is part of the reason I'm shifting to LA, and I have no desire to become the object of mother-daughter fervor here. My mum guilted me into meeting you, and though I admit you're better-looking than most of the girls I've seen, I'm a confirmed bachelor until I decide otherwise."

My mouth almost dropped open. How dare Tahir preempt my "I don't want to marry you" speech! "Well for your information, I don't want to marry you either! I'm an independent woman who doesn't believe in arranged marriage." Well one out of two wasn't bad.

For a split second I saw surprise flash across his eyes, but then it was gone. "Excellent," he said. "We understand each other. Now if you don't mind, I'm not up to walking to your car. Bring it around. I'll wait here."

My mouth tightened. Obviously Tahir was shy around the word "please." I opened my mouth to object, but fresh air and a few Tahir-free moments proved too tempting. "Fine." I whirled around and stalked out of the terminal.

Instead of feeling relieved that he'd effectively solved my problem for me, I was totally pissed off. His accent was sexy though. Tahir was a walking example that not every Indian immigrant sounded like a clerk at a 7-Eleven.

The sun had long since set. I scanned the area warily for rapists and muggers. LAX had pretty good security, but you never know. A safe male is a castrated male. I walked quickly to my car. The parking lot was brightly lit, but for some reason I felt uneasy. Meeting Tahir had obviously unnerved me.

I quickly disengaged the alarm and opened the door.

I wasn't fast enough.

An arm snaked around me from behind, and a sweet-smelling cloth was pressed to my nose and mouth. Before I could practice the Jackie Chan move I'd learned in self-defense class, the world disappeared.

And I faded into black.

Chapter 4

"NO, NO, I WANT a Coke. Pepsi is too sweet."

My lids were so heavy I could barely open them. The insides of my head ballooned with hideous hangover memories.

"No Coke. That's what I'm telling you. It's a common practice in America to carry one or the other."

It was an effort, but I opened my eyes. At first I thought I was in someone's bedroom, but then I saw a slight Indian man, dressed in a green windbreaker and jeans, rummaging through what was obviously a mini-bar.

That, along with the two double beds, tacky wall-paper, and a shoddy print of San Francisco Bay only a nearsighted person could appreciate, led me to the clever deduction that I was in a hotel room.

To my right another Indian man, older, with a full head of white hair, dressed in orange robes, peered du-biously over the rim of his glasses at a can of Pepsi.

"Who are you?" I had meant the question to come out

with authority, instead my voice croaked like one of Marge Simpson's sisters.

Both men turned and stared at me wide-eyed. "You have awoken," the man in the orange robes, said. "I humbly apologize for the chloroform. Pepsi?" He held out the can.

I was about to refuse or spit in his face, but my throat was absolutely parched. I reached for the can, and it was then that I realized my arms were tied to the chair.

Okay, this was scary.

Fear welled up inside of me, along with something else—

I was going to barf.

Some people scream when they're scared, some cry, I vomit. When I was six my parents enrolled me in swimming classes at the YMCA knowing I was deathly afraid of water. The swimming instructor was no more sympathetic. She blew her whistle and ordered me into the pool with the others. Two minutes later, she was blowing the whistle again, ordering everyone out. I stayed in while the remains of my breakfast floated around me. Swimming classes were never mentioned again.

I gagged. Saliva rushed into my mouth. I turned my head and spit onto the carpet. The younger man jumped up from the minibar and grabbed the trash can. He held it under my mouth. "Kindly project the contents here," he said politely.

I gagged again, looked at the trash can, then down at the pink cashmere Ralph Lauren top I was wearing. The risk of stains was too great. I shook my head. "I can hold it down."

The old man took a step forward. I pressed back into the seat. "Do not be afraid. You misunderstand. The restraints are not for your protection but for ours."

"*What?*"

"My name is Ramakrishna but you can call me Ram. I am from Calcutta. This is my cousin Sanjay. He lives in a city called Irvine."

"Hi," Sanjay said shyly. "I'm a software engineer. If you ever require help with Windows . . ."

Ram continued. "I belong to a sect that worships one deity and one deity only, Kali-Ma, the Dark Goddess."

"Right," I said and subtly continued to test my restraints.

"Unlike Lord Vishnu, who has resurrected numerous times as a fish, turtle, boar, lion, dwarf, Prince Ram, and Lord Krishna, to save the world from destruction, the goddess's rise had been foretold but never come to pass. Every night, for hundreds of years, the priests of our temple kept watch on the skies . . . until the miraculous happened. Thirty years ago a baby girl was born."

My legs were untied. If I lured the old man closer, I could get in a pretty good kick to the groin.

"This baby grew into a beautiful woman. A woman with the body of a lush lotus blossom, with a face as pure and lovely and radiant as the moon."

Ram knelt in front of me and winced. "Arthritis." He looked behind him, and Sanjay quickly got to his knees as well. "After numerous years and thousands of miles, I, your loyal servant, have come to deliver the joyous news that you are the one and only incarnation of the goddess Kali."

"Holy shit," I gasped.

"Yes," Ram said seriously.

Talk about dharma . . .

Chapter 5

AFTER THE INITIAL SHOCK of hearing I was a born-again goddess, my head cleared and I realized I was possibly in the company of two of the craziest men this side of the Himalayas. "I don't believe in reincarnation. How come everybody's a prince or princess in their past life? Someone had to have been a chambermaid or a dung beetle. Can you explain that?"

Ram adopted a very thoughtful expression and scratched his chin. "No, I cannot. I have not attained full enlightenment yet. When I reach that stage I will surely tell you the answer."

I rolled my eyes. "Can you at least get rid of these restraints? Or do I have to wait for you to attain Nirvana for that, too?"

"Do you promise not to slaughter us with the force of your divine wrath?"

I shrugged. "Sure."

Ram nodded to Sanjay, who quickly began untying the ropes. After they were removed I toyed with the idea of lunging at them with a leering face just to see if they were truly scared of me, but I was too exhausted.

Sanjay handed me my Kate Spade bag, and I made a quick examination to see if all the contents were there. M.A.C. compact, two M.A.C. lipsticks, one matte, one frost, cell phone, keys, wallet, and silver Mont Blanc pen. Check. "See you Hindu Smurfs later," I called, and made for the door.

Well, they were short.

"Please wait." Ram put out a hand to stop me. This time I was ready with the move and had him flat on his back in seconds. Sanjay quickly rushed over. "Please," Ram rasped. "Why do you refuse to believe you are Kali?"

I sighed and turned around, keeping my hand firmly on the doorknob. "Where do I start? I haven't been to the Cerritos Hindu Temple since I was, like, ten. In fact I'm not a religious person at all though I have been known to get down on my knees and thank God when Nordstrom has a sale."

Ram grimaced and moved to a chair with Sanjay's help. "There is a birthmark on your body, shaped like three dots. If you were to join them the figure would resemble a triangle."

A slight chill came over me. Wordlessly I pushed up the sleeve of my right arm and bared the mark on my shoulder. Three dots.

Sanjay stared wide-eyed and pointed. "There, she has it!"

Ram nodded in a bored way. "Yes, yes, naturally it is there. The mark represents your third eye, the eye of wisdom. Only Shiva and Kali have it. Have you ever been wounded? Seriously ill?"

I didn't need to think this one through. I'd never been one of those lucky kids who got to stay home from school because of chicken pox or the flu. In fact I'd never been injured in my life, not a bee sting, not a splinter, not even massive trauma to the head. I'd put it down to overprotective doctor parents, but now I wondered.

"No," I said finally.

Ram studied my face. "Let me ask you another question then. Have you ever felt vengeful?"

"Who hasn't? America's the lawsuit capital of the world," I pointed out, and went to sit on the bed. The birthmark thing sort of unnerved me, and I wanted to know more.

"An occasion when you felt anger so powerful it consumed you," Ram clarified.

"Well, there was the time my favorite show *Dark Shadows* was canceled but I wouldn't characterize myself as vengeful, more implacable."

"Are you sure she's the one?" Sanjay whispered loud enough for me to hear.

"The astrologer has never been mistaken," Ram whispered back.

I was about to tell the Abbott and Costello of the East that I could hear them when, as if summoned, a memory surfaced with startling clarity. "There was this one instance," I murmured.

Ram turned to me with an encouraging smile. "Tell us."

Chapter 6

I FELT LIKE a character in a bad movie who suddenly remembers incredibly vital information she somehow coincidentally forgot, until prodded, but that's how it was. After all, most people can explain away coincidences faster than Joan Rivers reaching for a Botox-laden syringe. "We'd just moved to Newport Beach," I began, "and some of the neighborhood kids started calling me Gandhi girl."

Sanjay handed me a bag of pretzels and a Pepsi from the minibar. "Kids can be cruel."

"And surprisingly knowledgeable about historical figures." I crossed my legs and flicked open the can of soda. "But what do you expect? When you bring chicken tandoori sandwiches to school and everyone else is packing bologna on white, you're bound to have some peer-adjustment problems."

A sharp ringing startled me into stopping. Sanjay reached inside his windbreaker and pulled out his cell phone. "Hello?" His face broke out into a huge smile. "Indira! No I'm not busy."

Ram cleared his throat, his face stern. "Sanjay."

Sanjay turned away and dropped his voice. "Friday then? It's a date." He hung up and straightened, shooting me an apologetic smile.

"Whatever." I shrugged and took a sip of Pepsi. "One day the kids were having a contest to see who could jump off the highest point. Determined to prove I was as good, if not better than they were, I shimmied up the side of our house, stood on the top of the garage and yelled, *'Hey losers! Did you know Gandhi could fly?'* They came running."

I paused to see if my audience was still paying attention, they were. "I was about to jump when I decided to do something a little more risky and pulled myself up until I was standing on top of our second-story roof. The kids were staring up at me with a mixture of fear and awe. This was my moment. I jumped and landed smoothly on the driveway."

A smile tugged at the corner of my mouth. "I became sort of a hero after that. I had full access to all the Atari games in the neighborhood."

Ram scratched his chin. With his protruding jaw, shock of white hair, and chocolate-colored skin, he resembled a wizened old monkey. "I see."

Obviously my story wasn't the heavenly example he was expecting. So maybe it didn't compare to Clark Kent twirling tractors at the age of five, but at least it was something. I jumped up. "Hey! That's a distance of like, twenty-five feet! No one can do that without protection and not get hurt, but that day I knew I could. It was weird."

"I think it sounds somewhat miraculous," Sanjay said in a comforting voice.

"Damn straight it does!" I was about to continue when it occurred to me my stance had changed from arguing why I wasn't a goddess to why I was. I shot Ram a suspicious look. He was smiling. I placed a hand on my hip and tossed back my hair. No one could do sassy and outraged better. "You tricked me!"

Ram blinked his eyes innocently. "The priests of my temple do not indulge in trickery."

I picked up my bag. "I don't know why I'm still here. This is all a mistake. Birthmark aside, you've got the wrong chick."

Ram opened his mouth to protest, but I held up my hand and silenced him. "In sixth grade Dana Padilla called my mom a clown because she picked me up from school dressed in a sari. Know what I did? I paid Stephanie Dawson, the tallest and widest girl in our class, twenty bucks to beat the shit out of Dana while I watched. Aren't divine beings supposed to be gentle and nurturing? I totally enjoyed watching Dana get her ass kicked, and that hardly sounds like the actions of a goddess."

Ram leaped to his feet, his voice booming out. "Not the actions of a goddess? Kali-Ma is the Goddess of Destruction! She is the bringer of death so that life may resurrect!" He threw out his arms. "Kali is womb and tomb, giver of life and devourer of her children."

I curled my lip. Devourer of her children? Didn't sound too appealing.

Ram's face was alight with joy and a feverish excitement. "The Dark Mother gives life to us all. Jai Ma Kali!"

"Long live mother Kali," Sanjay translated for me.

"I know what it means," I snapped. My bag suddenly felt like it weighed a ton. I wanted to go home and crawl into bed. "I'm leaving."

Ram quickly scribbled a number on the notepad provided by the hotel and tore off the sheet, handing it to me. "I cannot afford this lovely Holiday Inn room. I will be staying with Sanjay." He shot his cousin a disapproving sidelong glance. "Even though I have seen shanties in Bombay more accommodating than his flat." Sanjay's lower lip trembled, but Ram ignored it. "Please call me when you are ready for your lesson."

Lesson? I took the paper and stuffed it in my purse. Ram was getting quite adept at reading my expressions, and spoke up before I could leave. "You are still doubtful. Tomorrow after you are rested, go outside, close your eyes, and call the Goddess Within. See the power flowing up from your womb and radiating down from your third eye. You will have your proof."

"Your car is on parking level one, C2," Sanjay added, and handed me the ticket.

I was about to leave when the most obvious question struck me. "Wait, how'd you guys know I'd be at the airport today?"

"Sanjay was under strict orders to follow you around

until I arrived and ascertained you were indeed the *One*," Ram explained.

"You were following me?" I turned to Sanjay. "I didn't even see you."

Sanjay grabbed the bag of pretzels and popped one in his mouth. "It's fortunate you're Kali and thus protected from harm."

"Why?"

"Because"—he paused and grabbed another pretzel—"you're one god-awful driver."

Chapter 7

"TEN BUCKS," the thin, pimply-faced, male attendant said in a sleepy voice.

I handed over the bill and jammed out of the underground garage. I'd been kidnapped, drugged, and now I was getting screwed up the butt for parking.

On top of that Sanjay had rudely criticized my driving. Was that any way to treat a goddess? So what if I drove with my cell phone in one hand and a Frappuccino in the other? Most Southern Californians did the same.

I sped down Sepulveda Boulevard, miraculously free of airport traffic. This particular Holiday Inn was right next to LAX. So Ram and Sanjay didn't go very far.

I couldn't believe no one noticed two Indian men, one dressed in orange robes, smuggling an unconscious body into a car and out of the airport parking garage. I imagined Ram and Sanjay casually strolling through the hotel lobby, my comatose form propped up between them. Hadn't that rated at least one raised eyebrow from the concierge?

Because of the late hour, traffic in LA and Orange County proved relatively sparse. Forty-five minutes and I was home.

I stepped inside, expecting my parents to be up, demanding to know what happened to their only daughter. Instead the house was quieter than a cluster of nuns at a Marilyn Manson concert. Mom and Dad were obviously asleep.

Just as I reached my room, the guest bedroom door opened and the last person I expected to see stood there.

"What on Earth happened to you?" Tahir demanded. "Your parents were absolutely ill with worry. I offered to wait up so they could get some sleep."

I yawned. "That was nice."

"Not quite. I happen to be suffering from the most awful jet lag."

I slumped against the wall. "What are you doing here anyway? I thought you were staying with my aunt?"

"Thanks to your shockingly vulgar display of manners at the airport, I was forced to converse with a ruffian of a baggage handler on where to get a taxi. Public transportation is pathetic here. Your parents were understandably horrified to hear of my ordeal and kindly offered to let me stay."

I yawned again and felt my eyelids droop. "Well good night then."

"Excuse me," Tahir snapped. "I'm not quite finished."

I looked up and smiled. He was as beautiful as I remembered. "Kiss my brown ass."

Before he could respond another door opened and my parents stood there, tired and rumpled in their pajamas. My mom tucked a lock of black hair behind her ear. "Maya, where were you?"

Staring at their weary faces lined with concern, I longed to tell them the truth. Maybe they'd take the news their daughter was the incarnation of the goddess Kali by exchanging high fives and hugging each other.

After all, my decision not to major in premed had gone over pretty well. Mom had fainted twice, and Dad had faked a heart attack.

I just wasn't ready to share this particular news with anyone, not until I figured it out for myself.

I decided to resort to the excuse one of my high school friends, Lisa Kim, had used with her parents to great advantage. Facing them I took a deep breath. "Mom, Dad, it was terrible, there were these white supremacists and . . ."

Enough said.

Chapter 8

MY EYES OPENED at the crack of noon.

I blinked and spared a thought for the events of the night before. Goddess incarnate, please. It had taken me two months just to learn how to insert a tampon correctly.

I staggered out of bed and retrieved my purse from the floor. My cell phone fell out, and I winced at the number of missed calls, all from one number, home. I plugged it into the charger, then jumped in the shower. I wasn't sure my parents accepted my excuse from the night before. If I were going to face them, I'd do it feeling zestfully clean.

No one was home.

I checked the dry erase calendar in the kitchen where family members were supposed to record their daily schedules. My parents had duly filled out their whereabouts. Mom would be at her office until six, administering lollipops, diagnoses, and shots with equal aplomb to her young patients. Dad had a vasectomy scheduled for ten and something called a urologic oncology seminar from one to four.

Tahir was nowhere to be seen. Thank Vishnu for small favors!

I fixed myself a bagel and cream cheese, then thought, what the hell, and stuck a dollop of homemade, spicy, mint chutney on top like my dad was always telling me to. It was actually good.

Munching on my impromptu meal, I went through the house, out the French doors, and stepped barefoot onto the deck. The wood was pleasantly warm under my feet. To the right the pool gleamed and sparkled in the sunlight. I'd never seen either of my parents in a bathing suit, they'd never seen each other naked, and there wasn't a single copy of the Kama Sutra in our house.

To the left was my dad's garden filled with plump prizewinning roses. He'd told the neighbors the credit went to an ancient Indian gardening secret. His trick? Feeding them Budweiser beer.

I walked toward the edge of the pool. It was a beautiful day, mild, despite being the middle of January. The sky was a wide expanse of blue with a cloud dotted here and there to break the seemingly endless azure infinity.

I stuck out a toe and swirled the water. I wasn't about to swim. I did my laps at night. My golden complexion was natural, and I didn't want the risk of skin cancer, or worse, wrinkles.

Dusting my hands free of crumbs, I stuck out my right

arm. I was wearing a black GAP signature T-shirt, and
the birthmark on my shoulder was easily visible. Three
dots in the shape of a triangle.

Could I really be Kali?

Or what if this was some elaborate scam?

Ram kidnapped women all over the world, told them
they were goddesses in disguise, then hit them up for a
fat check, all in the name of divine duty. I'm sure if I'd
hung around the Holiday Inn a bit longer, he would've
started his spiel on how his temple really needed a bigger altar and for just a few thousand rupees more . . .

Still.

There was the matter of my birthmark. And Ram's description of a young woman with the body of a lush lotus
blossom pretty much fit me to a tee.

Meanwhile, there was definitely one thing I could do.

Time to do a little research on the dark goddess Kali.

Chapter 9

INDIA IS CONSIDERED the bastion of spirituality. Every mountaintop is supposedly sprinkled with wise men in orange robes contorting themselves into complex yogic positions or communing with trees. So just because I share the same ethnic heritage as those men doesn't mean I have some inborn sense of the metaphysical.

At the age of ten I'd taken a stand to stop attending the Cerritos Hindu Temple with my family. There were far more important things than learning the origins and teachings of one of the world's oldest religions, namely, Sunday morning cartoons.

Not that it really mattered; I was pretty much failing Hinduism 101. It was the pundit's fault. He should've taken my suggestion to put epics like the Mahabharat and Ramayan in comic book form. As a result I could barely tell the difference between Vishnu and Shiva.

Of course I'd heard of Kali, along with gods like Ganesh and Hanuman. However, with regard to the second two, I couldn't remember which one was a monkey and which had the head of an elephant.

I went back through the house and into what, according to the real estate agent, was supposed to be the library. My parents had converted it into a Puja room, where they laid garlands, burned incense, and offered coconuts to the Hindu gods on a white marble altar. I didn't have any coconuts on me, but I did put half of a Twix on the offering plate.

There were several deities my family worshipped, and as I gazed at the statuettes, some of it began to come back. The flute-playing man in blue was Krishna, probably the most famous incarnation of the god Vishnu. He'd definitely set the bar high for future divine embodiments like me. Krishna's teachings were summed up in the Bhagavad Gita, sort of the Hindu Bible.

Next to Krishna was Lakshmi, seated in a yogic position on top of a lotus blossom, her lovely face a perfect picture of serenity. Lakshmi was the Goddess of Wealth so I said a quick prayer over my Lotto numbers.

I was surprised to see two non-Hindu icons. A bronze Buddha in the laughing pose and a small, framed painting of Guru Nanak, the founder of Sikhism. Apparently my parents were more open-minded than I thought.

Now if they'd only get off my back about marriage.

The last statue was of a chubby god with an elephant head. Staring at his appealing face I remembered he was

Ganesh, the remover of obstacles. I said a quick prayer to him over my Lotto numbers, too.

Lakshmi was the only female featured on the altar, so my parents obviously didn't worship Kali. This was a dead end. There was another place I could try, though, and they happened to serve Starbucks coffee.

Chapter 10

DESPITE THE FACT it was Monday afternoon, the two-story Barnes & Noble bookstore was doing steady business. Students and shoppers occupied all the tables in the café. I opted for a Venti Caramel Macchiato and, sipping my drink, headed toward the escalator. Religion was on the second floor. An accident or direct attempt to put the section closer to the heavens?

I passed by the information desk where a heavyset blond woman was arguing with a harried male clerk. "But the book was there last week, and now it's gone!"

"Do you know the title or author?" the clerk asked.

The woman pursed her lips. "No. But it had a purple cover."

Leaving the clerk to the delights of customer service, I let the escalator carry me up, up and away.

I got off next to the political science section and had to walk to the opposite end of the floor to find religion. The bookstore was clearly adhering to the separation of church and state.

I started on one end of the aisle and began working my way down. There were three full shelves on Christianity, one shelf on Judaism, and a third of a shelf for Hinduism, Buddhism, and Islam.

Hmm, talk about your Holy War.

I plucked three titles on Hinduism off the shelf, then had to circle the floor several times before nabbing a corner table vacated by two students wearing UCI sweatshirts.

I took a revitalizing sip of my drink and cracked open the first book. Scanning the table of contents I found the page number, flipped to the chapter on Kali, and began reading.

Kali, the black goddess, is naked with long matted hair. She wears severed arms as a girdle, a necklace of freshly cut heads, children's corpses as earrings and cobras as bracelets.

Umm . . .

I didn't know if it was the mint chutney, but an uncomfortable stirring had begun in my stomach.

Okay maybe it was just the author's bias that made Kali sound like Lakshmi's ugly stepsister. I took another fortifying sip of my coffee, and turned to a different page.

Kali has long sharp fangs and claw-like hands. Her hangouts include the battlefield, where, as the fiercest of all warriors, she gets drunk on the blood of her victims or, in a cremation ground, where she is surrounded by jack-als and goblins.

Yuck!

The stirring in my stomach had become a churning.

There were a few things Ram had neglected to tell me about Kali, namely, her freakish fashion sense. If I were Kali's personal shopper I'd dress her in Dolce & Gabbana, and advise leaving the necklace of freshly cut heads at home.

I needed to see a picture. Quick.

I picked up another book and turned a few pages until I came upon one. I studied it for a few moments, then cocked my head and considered it from another angle.

Personally, I didn't see what was so scary about the goddess Kali. So her red protruding tongue contrasted with her ink black skin, and yeah, she was juggling a trio of human heads, and had teeth that would put Dracula to shame but . . .

I slammed the book shut.

Pushing back my chair, I grabbed my purse and ran to the bathroom. Thankfully it was empty. I stood in front of the mirror. My reflection stared back at me. Flawless oval face, smooth black brows that arched perfectly to frame my almond-shaped brown eyes, full lips, long black hair . . .

I held up my slender hands—definitely not claw-shaped. And I would never drink blood, not even if it were guaranteed to make me lose weight. Plus there weren't any cremation grounds in Orange County that I knew of, but if there were, you wouldn't find me partying it up there on a Saturday night.

The blenderlike movements in my stomach subsided a bit.

I returned to the table, which was, of course, occupied, and grabbed a different book. I leaned against a shelf of Stephen King novels, appropriate for the subject matter and flipped pages until I came to another picture. This time Kali was shown straddling a pale, white, male form. The caption read:

> *The Dark Mother, squatting over her dead consort Shiva and devouring his entrails, while her yoni sexually devours his lingam (penis).*

Gross!

And, technically, it'd been more than a year since my yoni had sexually devoured any lingam.

I tossed the book onto an empty cart and stepped over a little boy sprawled in the aisle, busy drooling over pictures in the *Joy of Sex*. He looked up and stared at me defiantly.

I wasn't about to steer him toward the Newbery Award winners, and left the little pervert stewing in his hormones. There were bigger things to think about. Namely, Kali was a horrifying creature who looked more like the Incredible Hulk than Wonder Woman. I couldn't be her, could I?

Considering the state my stomach was in, I tossed my coffee into the trash can. I'd also stop off at the drugstore for some Tums, just in case.

There was one surefire way to settle this once and for all.

It was time to do that womb-tomb mediation thing Ram had told me about.

Chapter 11

POPPING TUMS LIKE CANDY, I drove down Newport Boulevard, traffic parting before me faster than the Red Sea for Moses. My dad referred to me in my H2 as a weapon of mass destruction.

Ram said to try the exercise outside. For obvious reasons I didn't think the Barnes & Noble parking lot would suffice, I knew a far more suitable place.

I turned onto Iris Avenue, heading toward a small, secluded section of Corona del Mar beach. It was practically deserted, and I parked on the shoulder of the road. On the weekend both sides of the street would be lined with cars.

Slipping out of my Tommy Bahama sandals, I scooped them up in one hand and stepped onto the sand. I walked toward the water's edge, and looked around surreptitiously, but this area of the beach was empty—no body surfers, no bobbing bosoms in bikinis, no bloated bodies burning brightly.

Ram said to close my eyes and visualize the energy

flowing up from my womb and down from my third eye. Too bad I had no idea where either spot was. Was my third eye between my eyebrows or slightly above?

According to my birthmark it was slightly above, like a pyramid. Now where the hell was my womb? Would the stomach region suffice? Maybe I'd focus on my uterus? Thanks to Aunt Gayatri, I knew exactly where that was.

I closed my eyes and began to chant "Om." I was playing by ear, and *Om* seemed as good a word as any. Personally, I doubted I'd experience anything other than a few relaxing yogic breaths.

"Ommm." I stretched the syllable out as far as I could. Other than the call of seagulls in the distance, the beach was relatively silent. The Pacific Ocean truly lived up to her name. Waves eased onto the shore with barely a whisper.

I took another deep breath and imagined energy as a golden hand, traveling up from the nether reaches of my body, and down from my forehead, connecting as two fingertips in my chest.

Okay, so I stole the idea from Michelangelo.

I did this a few times, staring hard at the insides of my eyelids, and saw nothing except for the usual swirls of geometric colors. Moments passed.

Zilch.

I opened my eyes and exhaled. It hadn't worked. Had I expected it to? But it wasn't like I had any pressing matters to attend to, so I tried again.

Nada.

My eyes flew open and I kicked at the sand. This was ridiculous!

I wasn't one of those people who crossed over with John Edward or happily panted with the Pet Psychic. I didn't scamper through the woods looking for fairies or roam the desert trying to contact E.T. I believed in the tangible, like credit cards. But here I was, trying to summon up cosmic energy from my fallopian tubes.

I suppose I could have continued being disgusted with myself, but that wasn't any fun. Instead, I channeled my anger against Ram. What right did he have to disrupt my life this way? I was going to drop-kick him on the side of the head. I was going to run over his bony ass in my megaton SUV.

Righteously pissed, I threw out my arms and shouted, "Om!"

And something happened . . .

A pool of warmth began building in my stomach. Like soft liquid lava it traveled up, spread through my chest, rushed along my arms, and seeped down into my legs. The point between my eyes began tingling. With a shaking hand I pressed the tip of my finger there. It burned.

A shadow fell across my face, and my eyes drifted upward. The blue sky was spreading with black.

Oh-my-God!

Chapter 12

A FIERCE WIND, warm and carrying the scent of a faraway land, sprang up and lashed out at the smooth surface of the ocean, kicking the water into massive, churning waves. My long hair swirled around me like a shawl of black silk.

Lightning strikes laced through the darkness, and the warmth inside me seethed into pure intense power. My nerve endings were buzzing.

The wind swelled with hurricane force. It was all I could do to keep on standing, but I felt better than I ever had in my life. Laughter spilled from my mouth, and the wind carried the sound until it echoed all around me.

I was sheer energy. I was light.

I was invincible.

Then, like tendrils of a venomous creeper, an image of Kali I'd glimpsed in one of the books slowly spread through my mind. Dark, fierce, holding a bloodstained sword in one hand, and a decapitated man's head in the other. Threads of cartilage hung where his neck used to be.

"No!"

My hands fell to my side. In haste, I jumped back from the water and fell hard against the sand. "Stop!" I didn't know who or what I was talking to.

I only hoped someone was listening.

My adrenaline rush of atomic proportions was swallowed up by sheer panic. What if I'd opened some sort of Pandora's box? What if I'd unleashed an unstoppable force?

But the wind died down to nothing, the sky cleared, and the surface of the water was once again calm.

Whoa.

If Starbucks bottled a jolt like that, they'd make millions.

Oh right, they already had.

Hours passed, and the sun hovered along the rim of blue. I continued to sit, watching the water gently caress the sand. I didn't try the womb-tomb exercise again. There were now some scattered surfers paddling out into the ocean, and I didn't think they'd appreciate tsunami-force waves, even if they did manage to catch the ride of their lives, literally.

The more I thought about what happened, the less strange it began to feel. It wasn't just the surreal nature of it all. With that power inside me, everything had felt so—right. Like all the pieces inside of me finally clicked together.

God, I was starting to sound like New Age guru Deepak Chopra. But maybe people like Deepak had it right? There was another world beyond this world. A world I had neither seen nor believed existed, until now.

Besides, there was a Mehra family reunion coming up in a few months, and I was curious about what else I could do.

Standing, I dusted the sand from my jeans and slowly walked back to the car. Retrieving my purse from the passenger seat, I pulled out my cell phone along with the paper Ram had given me and began dialing.

Oprah always said every woman was a goddess . . .

As the phone began to ring, I knew exactly what I was going to ask Ram first—

How much did this job pay anyway?

Chapter 13

RAM WANTED to meet immediately.

I called home, left a message on the answering machine that I was having dinner with a friend, and hung up. Both my parents had cell phones but I wasn't about to call them and deal with potential questions. Tonight, Mom, Dad, and their guest could have a nice quiet dinner without me. Sooner or later Tahir would criticize the food or the furniture, and my parents would see the man for the ass he was.

Around seven I pulled up outside the Woodbridge apartment complex in Irvine. Ram was waiting outside, wearing orange robes as usual. I imagined he had quite a few of them hanging in his closet.

With anticipation I watched him approach the car. What was going to happen next? What would he teach me? He took a seat, and I caught a whiff of sandalwood. He'd also added a necklace of wooden beads.

"Where to?" I asked.

"Sanjay says there is a very good restaurant just down the lane. Why not go there?"

Not exactly the exciting beginning I'd imagined, but I was the student, and he was the teacher. I drove slowly down the street, keeping an eye out for restaurants.

"There! There!" He pointed excitedly. "That is the one!"

The familiar neon sign featured two words. I turned to him. "You can't be serious. Taco Bell?"

"Yes, yes, it is Sanjay's favorite place."

"Okay . . ."

I parked and we walked inside. Ram gazed around the fluorescent fast-food establishment beaming, his sandals making a *clip-clop* sound on the linoleum floor. All around us people stared. I stared fixedly back, and most of them looked away.

He gazed up at the oversized menu screen, rubbing his hands gleefully. "What to have? Oh what to have?"

I'd never seen anyone this excited over Taco Bell before.

Ram looked over his shoulder and a thoughtful expression crossed his face. "I shall reserve a table. You will please order the food."

I guess we knew who was paying. "Sure," I said, and watched as he walked from table to occupied table, and eventually stopped beside a couple that looked like they were halfway through dinner. They glanced up and Ram smiled.

"Uh, we're not exactly done yet," the guy said.

"Please take your time." Ram's smile grew even wider. "I will sit only when you are through."

The girl's eyes traveled from his full head of white hair, down to his wrinkled face, and even farther down to his sandal-clad feet. "We're done," she said and stood up with the tray.

"Thank you. You are most kind." Still smiling, Ram took her vacated seat.

For a moment the guy stubbornly continued to sit there. "Come on," the girl insisted. Grumbling, he threw down his burrito and followed her.

Ram waved at me, and I found myself smiling and waving back. The priests of his temple had kept watch on the skies for thousands of years, waiting for my birth. A couple halfway through dinner at Taco Bell did not pose a problem.

When it was my turn to order, I decided to get one of every vegetarian item on the menu. I had no idea what Ram would like and figured he might as well try everything. At the last minute I ordered a Nacho Bell Grande for myself, without meat, in case he wanted a bite.

Hefting the fully packed tray, I grabbed thirty packets or so of hot sauce from the bin, because bland food comes right after malaria on India's list of things to be avoided at all cost, and made my way over to the table.

"*Bon appétit*," I said.

Ram reached for his drink and took a long sip. Grimacing, he stuck out his tongue. "This is Pepsi. I wanted Coke."

"Taco Bell only has Pepsi."

"Pepsi is too sweet."

"I know. I prefer Coke myself."

He sighed. "I am having a very serious Pepsi problem in this country."

There wasn't much conversation for the next thirty minutes, other than Ram holding up a quesadilla or tostada and asking me what it was called. "This is my favorite," he said, taking a bite out of a seven-layer burrito. "What is this green sauce?"

I glanced over. "Guacamole. It's made from avocado."

"Delicious."

"If you like, I can make it for you fresh. Guacamole is one thing I do well." Maybe in the future I could add saving the world from destruction to that list.

"Yes please." Ram popped the last bite of the burrito in his mouth, sat back, and let out a huge belch. A few kids next to us began giggling. Ram winked and smiled at them.

"About the lesson," I began.

Ram sat up. "Yes, we will begin."

"Great." I stood up.

"We will do it here."

"Here?" I sat back down. "In Taco Bell?"

"It is a most wonderful place, is it not?"

"I don't know. I guess."

"We need to be in a place with many people."

It looked like we were staying. I'd long since finished my nachos and reached for a bean-and-cheese burrito Ram had left untouched. "Okay, so what's the lesson?"

"First, what have you learned regarding Kali-Ma?"

"Well," I chewed thoughtfully, "everything about her is so eww."

Ram frowned. "What is the meaning of this eww?"

"She's nasty, Ram. Why's she always shown curling up to severed body parts?"

"Kali is the Dravidian She-Goddess," he began patiently.

"Dravidian She-Ogre is more like it."

Ram cleared his throat and fixed me with a stern look over the rim of his glasses. No longer was he the burrito-loving swami. "The essence of divinity is the absence of fear. That is Kali-Ma. That is why she is shown in the cremation ground, why she surrounds herself with blood and gore. She is bound with the terrifying, and she is unafraid. She is divine."

I squirted some more hot sauce on my burrito. "You know, I've always considered myself pretty divine, too."

"The battle to save the world will be fought between the divine and antidivine forces."

"Antidivine, meaning evil?"

Ram nodded. "Evil is always based on fear and, therefore, not divine."

"I've been wanting to ask you. Why didn't I show any signs of being a goddess earlier? You know, like zapping my trigonometry teacher to the darkest corners of the universe or something?"

Ram stared at me puzzled. "Why would you do that to your teacher?"

"Why wouldn't I?"

"A woman does not attain her full shakti until the age of thirty."

"Shakti?" I knew that was Sanskrit for feminine power or energy.

"You would not have been able to call the Goddess Within, until your thirtieth birthday. Now you are at full shakti."

I wondered what the fashion magazines would say to that? Considering they subscribed to the idea that a woman peaked at eighteen. "I'm ready. What do I do?"

Ram pushed the tray away and rested his arms on the table. "Call the Goddess Within as you did earlier. Focus on the energy moving inside you."

I recalled the storm I had summoned. "I can't do that here," I hissed. "Taco Bell wrappers will be flying all over the place, not to mention Taco Bell customers."

"What you do not choose to happen, will not happen," Ram replied firmly.

He did have a point. When I'd wanted everything to return to normal, it had, immediately. I nodded. "Okay, do I need to do anything besides that?"

"Stare at the people around you."

"What am I looking for?"

"Malevolence."

Malevolence? Who didn't feel malevolent after ingesting a few fifty-nine-cent tacos? What if I confused it with heartburn? "How will I recognize malevolence?"

"You will know. It is what you are meant to do. Recognize evil and stop it."

I closed my eyes and took a deep breath.

Here we go again.

Chapter 14

THIS TIME I didn't chant.

I began the process of visualizing and immediately the liquid warmth spread through my body. The spot above my eyebrows began to tingle, but the sensation was almost pleasant.

"You are radiant. The goddess has awoken," Ram murmured. "Open your eyes and gaze at those around you."

I turned and slowly skimmed the room. At first I thought my vision had blurred. There were fuzzy halos of light surrounding everyone. Then it occurred to me what I was actually seeing.

Wow, people really did have auras!

I couldn't believe that the frizzy-haired lady at the metaphysical mall, who kept trying to force her crystals on me, was right.

I focused closely on the unusual light.

The kids who had giggled at Ram's belching, along with other taco-loving tots, had colored auras, and each provoked a different emotion in me. Green auras emitted a sense of peace, red triggered energy and excitement. A few adults had color, too, some brighter than others. The rest had auras tinged with gray, from them, I felt nothing.

Slowly the realization dawned on me. Those with colored auras still had life in them. The brighter the color, the more life I could feel. It made sense that all the kids still had color, at that age life pulsed with possibilities.

But the gray auras far outnumbered the rest.

No wonder self-help books were such hot sellers. Maybe I could write one titled, "Turn your gray aura blue" or something like that?

My Malevolent Meter was quiet though.

Taco Bell was free of evil.

I turned to Ram. A brilliant bright yellow surrounded him. He oozed sunshine and happiness. The man was a walking Hallmark card! I almost had to reach for my sunglasses.

But what did my aura look like? I opened my purse, this time a striped Fendi with sharp silver buckles, and pulled out a compact.

Wait.

What exactly would I see?

I couldn't help it, a small sliver of fear embedded itself in my brain. If I looked in the mirror, would I see Kali's face instead of mine?

Straightaway, the warmth inside me began to dissipate.

Ram watched me intently. "Something is wrong."

"Nothing's wrong. I didn't feel any malevolence though. Too bad, huh?"

"Something happened when you reached for your purse."

"I remembered I left my favorite lip gloss at home."

Ram was stubborn as a schnauzer and opened his mouth to argue.

I picked up our tray and stood up. "Let's go. I'm starting to smell like refried beans."

Outside, the temperature had dropped considerably, and I shivered in my T-shirt. Hurrying to the car, I unlocked the doors and jumped in. "So did I do the exercise wrong? I feel like those monkeys—see no evil, hear no evil."

Ram climbed into his seat and struggled with the seat belt. "Now that you have awoken the Goddess Within, there is no way you cannot recognize evil. It is your dharma, the reason you were born."

I took his seat belt, locked it into place, and started the car. "Did anyone ask me about that? I would've preferred my dharma to be a little more like Julia Roberts's."

"It was your choice. It always is," Ram said simply.

I roared out of the parking lot and cut in front of two cars. I noticed Ram clutching the sides of the seat. Maybe he wasn't used to the way Americans drove on the right.

I took my eyes off the road and turned to Ram. His whole body tensed. "About this evil-stopping business . . . am I supposed to stare malevolence down with my nifty third eye? Offer up a free aura reading?"

Ram's voice was unusually high-pitched. "Does not a red light indicate you must stop?"

"What?" I turned back to the road and slammed on the brakes. We screeched to a halt. I stretched and yawned. Ram looked positively green. Maybe I shouldn't have let him eat all that fast food, it obviously didn't agree with him.

In moments we were back in front of Sanjay's apartment building. Ram practically clawed at the door handle and leaped out. He was trembling for some reason, but managed a smile. "Find the courage to trust your talents."

"You mean the talent I just found out last night I have?" I gripped the steering wheel. "There's so much evil in the world. Do I hop on a plane and take out the nearest dictator or start with the crime around here? I mean, the murder rate in LA alone could keep me busy for decades."

"You will know what to do when the time comes," Ram said. "Until then, just be."

"How wonderfully cryptic. Did I mention Yoda is my least favorite character of all time?"

Ram waved cheerily. "Good night. We will talk tomorrow."

I pulled away from the curb. So according to Ram, and he had a pretty good track record with the truth, my soul had volunteered to save the world from the forces of evil.

That made sense. I was quite the impulsive shopper. I'm sure my soul figured this particular dharma deal sounded pretty cool and glamorous. I bit my lip. Life wasn't a 50-percent-off sale. But if it were, I was having the most critical case of buyer's remorse ever.

Chapter 15

MY GAS-GUZZLER of a tank was nearly empty, and I pulled into a Chevron station near the entrance to the 405 freeway. Thankfully the gas station was deserted, and I didn't have to listen to any male comments like, "What's a little girl like you doin' in a big car like that?"

I had my comeback though. "What's a small brain like yours doin' in a big head like that?"

The response was invariably the same and delivered with a sneer. "Bitch."

I swiped my credit card, slipped in the nozzle, then leaned back against my car to wait. I could have a mini-nap in the time it took for my H2 to fill up. Deeming it unwise, however, to nap at a gas station late at night, with my purse sitting on the front seat, I instead thought back to the events of the day.

Why wasn't I more Bellevue about all this? Shouldn't I be on the shrink's sofa, drooling into my neck? I had no way of knowing since there was hardly a support group for people like me. Harry Potter had a whole school of his peers. All I had was Ram.

Maybe my reaction was normal? A lifetime spent playing video games and watching movies made the unreal acceptable.

Hey! What if my life were a video game! A potential fortune lay with Nintendo. I didn't think of myself as greedy, but if I was supposed to save the world, shouldn't I at least be able to turn lead into gold or something? I mean, it was just—

Ugh!

An invisible blow landed on my stomach with enough force to knock me out. But no one was there, and I was still standing.

Ugh!

There it went again. Uneasiness crawled up my back. The weight pressed against my chest and stomach. I could barely breathe.

I knew what was happening. It couldn't be anything else.

I turned around.

Behind me two men were walking into the convenience store.

The malevolence radiated off them.

Ram was right. I would *know* evil.

The weight continued to press against me.

Dharma-fulfilling time.

Shit! Shit! Shit!

Chapter 16

THIS WAS NEW TERRITORY for me, and I thought about calling 911. But what would I tell the operator? "Umm, I just felt a really big pang in my chest . . . which sorta indicates evil's around, and I'm a pretty reliable source being that I'm a goddess so . . ."

I decided to follow them in.

The clerk behind the counter saw me enter, but the two goons didn't. They were too busy grabbing beers from the cooler. I moved past the magazines and dropped down in a crouching position behind one of the aisles, my face pressed against a packet of beef jerky.

From that vantage point I could see the front, but no one could see me. I peered around the corner and the clerk, a middle-aged man with olive skin and an Errol Flynn mustache, stared right at me with a puzzled expression. Quickly, I ducked back behind the jerky. Okay, so I wasn't as unobtrusive as I thought.

I waited a few moments, but the clerk didn't come down the aisle after me. Apparently a woman who wanted to get up close and personal with dried-up meat was no big deal. This was the night shift at a convenience store after all. There was probably someone masturbating in the bathroom right now.

I peeked around the corner again. The two men were at the counter. I got a good look at them from behind and summed up their appearance: saggy-assed.

One guy was white with a shaved head, his thick neck partially covered by the curling edge of a tattoo. A scorpion was my guess, but I wasn't about to ask him to remove his shirt so I could see the design. The other guy was dark, Hispanic-looking, his hair pulled back in a braid. He had tattoos, too, mostly of evil-eyed eagles.

Two tattooed thugs. How clichéd could you get?

The Latino lawbreaker shoved the carton of beer across the counter, and said in a low, intimidating growl, "Empty the cash register. Fast." His eyes narrowed as the clerk grabbed a plastic bag and began unloading. "I know where the button is, *hombre*. Don't even think of pushing it and calling the cops."

I sat back against the shelf. I should have called the Goddess Within outside, then entered the store. I should have taken my chance with the 911 operator. I should have bought Microsoft stock back in 1986.

I could cry over my regrets on my deathbed. Time to summon the goddess.

Closing my eyes, I took a deep breath, and—

"Well, look at this!" A rough hand closed down on the

soft part of my upper arm. My eyes flew open. Dragged
to my feet, I found myself face-to-face with the white,
hairless hooligan.

I definitely preferred the view from the back.

His eyes were the color of thick phlegm, his face a
blotchy red. He also happened to have the wispiest
goatee I'd ever seen. My grandmother had more hairs on
her chin when she went a day without plucking.

I struggled to free my arm. "Let go of me!"

Instead of obliging, he tightened his already bruising
grip and pulled me to the front of the store. "Check out
this bitch." He raked his eyes over my body from head to
toe. "What do I do with her?"

The braided brute's eyes never left the clerk. "Make
sure she don't call the cops."

Mr. Waste of Anatomy—seriously, where were organ
thieves when you needed them—grabbed my other arm
and pulled both roughly behind my back. If only I'd
worn my new steel-heeled stilettos, I could've stepped
back and sliced off his toe.

Oh right, the goddess thing.

I closed my eyes, took a deep breath and—

BOOM!

A massive gunshot ricocheted through the store. My
eyes flew open to see the Hispanic heavy glaring at the
clerk, smoking gun pointed at the ceiling. "Faster!"

The gunshot momentarily surprised the Big Nasty
breathing down my neck, and he loosened his grip.
Quickly, I kicked back and caught him squarely in the

knee. Cursing, he let go of one of my arms, and I hefted my bag and swung it at his face.

One of the sharp silver buckles caught him in the eye. He howled.

I pulled away and ran, trying to summon the goddess, but it was slightly difficult to visualize anything under the circumstances. All I could think about was getting away and calling the police.

I was almost to the door when my pursuer tackled me and we went flying into a rack of Twinkies and Ding Dongs. The baked goods were stale and did nothing to cushion my fall.

He whipped me around so we were again face-to-face. His hot fetid breath nearly made me black out. Talk about a serious Altoid moment.

I had just the one self-defense move, and it only worked when the person I wanted to flip was polite enough to stand across from me.

There was only one thing to do.

Fight like a girl.

I screamed like a maniac and went for his eyes, lashing out with my sharp, manicured nails.

Shaved head's thug-in-crime turned, brandishing his gun at me. "What the fuck's going on?"

I didn't know if I was impervious to bullets, and I didn't want to find out.

The thick-necked troglodyte rose to his feet, pulling me up painfully by my roots. My follicles screamed for José Eber.

I cried out, but not loud enough to miss the grate of metal against metal.

Click. Click.

The convenience store clerk stood there, legs spread, a rifle in each hand. "Let her go, or I'll blow both your bastard brains to Karachi."

Both men froze, gaping.

Wordlessly I was released, my ass making contact with a heap of Hostess cakes.

"In the corner, bastards," the clerk ordered. The legally challenged losers moved and stood, glaring.

I stared up at my hero. "Thanks."

The clerk nodded, putting one rifle on the counter and keeping the other trained on the robbers. "I've pushed the button to activate the alarm. The bastard cops will be here in thirty minutes."

"Thirty minutes?" I gasped.

He shrugged. "This happens three or four times a week."

I scrambled to my feet. The clerk surveyed me. "Are you Indian?"

"Yeah." I looked closely at his name tag. It read: ALI. "Are you?"

"Pakistani."

"My mom was born in Pakistan, before India was split up."

"Do you know where?"

"Lahore."

"I was born there, too."

The bald bandit curled his lip. "Damn immigrants."

Ali leveled his rifle. "Shut up, bastard. If not for immigrants like me, you bastards would have no one to rob."

The dark-skinned robber nudged his friend. "Hey, asshole, my family's from Mexico."

"They are?"

Well my work there was done.

I removed a piece of Twinkie from my hair. "Do you want me to stick around, Ali? Talk to the cops?"

"No." He waved me away. "I know how to handle their bastard questions."

"Thanks again." I headed for the door, giving the two men in the corner a well-deserved finger.

"Is that your Hummer outside?" Ali said.

"Yeah," I said proudly.

"You owe me forty dollars."

Oh, right, the gas. I smiled sheepishly and whipped out my wallet.

The white thug snorted. "What's a little girl like you doin' in a big car like that?"

I opened my mouth.

Forget it.

Chapter 17

I HAD TO CLEAR my throat several times before anyone noticed I was in the room.

My mom was the first to react. "Maya, you're back. We just finished eating." The table was scattered with remnants of dinner: a half-empty tureen of lentil soup or dal, a plate of chapattis, a nearly devoured vegetable dish of cauliflower and potatoes, heavily seasoned with black pepper, cumin, cardamom, nutmeg, cloves, and cinnamon. A bottle of wine rested in the center.

Wine?

My parents never drank wine. Occasionally my dad indulged in a scotch and soda before dinner, and my mom would nurse a rum and Coke (only at parties mind you), but wine?

Tahir poured a glass and set it down across from him. "Here, have a taste, Maya. It's an Australian wine, Shiraz. The selection at the shop was excellent."

"I like it," my mom said with a fond smile at Tahir. Her cheeks were tinged pink.

My dad was shoveling food into his mouth and barely nodded at me as I took a seat. He was wearing his favorite T-shirt with the logo: *Urologists do it in a cup.*

What I really wanted was a shower. I smelled like skinhead.

But I was never one to turn down wine.

I took a sip, and I couldn't keep a sound of pleasure from escaping my lips. Shiraz, huh? Merlot had just gone down a notch in my opinion.

Then Tahir smiled, and the wine nearly shot out of my mouth. The man should be prohibited from smiling. The effect was indecently attractive.

"You know your wines," he said. It was a statement, not a question.

I suppose if "knowing" wines meant consuming them to great extent, then I did. "I know what I like."

Tahir was staring at me. I found this disconcerting. I preferred him rude. He moved to top off my glass, which had somehow emptied itself. I took a sip and chanced another look over.

Tahir's eyes were still fixed on my face.

"Pass the dal," my dad said. I nearly jumped, forgetting he was there. Tahir really had me unsettled, or maybe it was the fact that, hours earlier, I had turned the sky black with my divine power? I passed the bowl, and my dad poured a few spoonfuls over his rice. "Did anyone notice the strange weather today?"

I nearly spit out my wine again. "No," I said a little too loudly.

My mom shook her head. "I was in the office all day."

Tahir scratched the side of his mouth. "Oh, you mean the momentary darkness and wind. Is that unusual for Southern California?"

My dad's attention was back on the food, and he didn't answer.

My mom dabbed gently at the corners of her mouth with a napkin. "We're going to Gayatri's tomorrow night. She's throwing a dinner party in honor of Tahir. Actually," she amended, "the party's in honor of both of you."

I took another sip, then realized she was looking at me. For the third time, I nearly spewed wine. This was too much. I downed the glass. "What? Me? Both of us?" I looked at Tahir. He was sitting back in his chair, facing me with a challenging expression. He hadn't told my parents! He was obviously waiting for me to do it, so I would look like the bad guy.

Asshole.

I lifted my chin, determined. "How nice of her. I'm sure the party will be fun."

Tahir's expression didn't change.

My mom smiled happily, completely unaware of the complex interplay of emotions across the table.

"Pass the chapattis," my dad grunted.

Okay, maybe not all the emotions were that complex.

I passed the chapattis. I wanted a hot shower, then bed. It wasn't that late, especially since I'd woken up at noon, but I was exhausted. I pushed back my chair. "Well it's good night for me."

No response.

My dad was still involved with his food, and my mom sat in her chair, a dreamy smile on her face. Looking at her I knew the state was partly due to the wine, but mostly due to images of the grandchildren she mistakenly believed Tahir and I would dutifully produce.

I glanced over at the man who'd supposedly supply the genetic half of our progeny. Tahir was quiet with his own thoughts, his thumb slowly tracing the rim of his wineglass. There was something so sensuous about the movement. His thumb made contact with a droplet of wine, embedding the juice deep into his skin. If I were to taste—

"What time will you wake?" Tahir said.

I snapped out of it, praying my expression was bland as a schoolmarm's. "I don't know, early. Maybe eight?" Everyone at the table looked at me. "Well that's early for me," I said defensively.

"What time do the shops open?" he asked.

"Nine."

"There are a few things I need to buy."

My mom jumped in. "What a wonderful idea! Maya can take you shopping, then the two of you can stop somewhere and have lunch? How about Las Brisas? Maya always goes there. Lunch will be on me."

"Excellent," Tahir said.

"Fine," I said flatly.

"Don't oversleep," Tahir called out, as I exited the room.

It was a good thing none of them heard my reply.

* * *

I lay in bed staring up at the ceiling. I'd been in the hot steamy shower for an hour, scrubbing my skin with a loofah, using the strongest scented bath gel I had. Afterward I'd rubbed my favorite Victoria's Secret body oil into my skin until I felt fresh and sweet.

Now I was lying in bed, blow-dried and bathed, and I still didn't feel clean. I knew what the problem was.

Tonight, I had failed.

Finally, for the first time in my life, there was something I was supposedly good at, something I was born to do, and I had failed. Without the rifle-wielding Ali, I don't know what would have happened to either one of us. I didn't want to think about it. My cheeks were crisscrossed with warm rivulets of tears before I even realized I was crying.

My mind drifted back to another time when I had cried in the dark, feeling like a failure.

When I was twelve, my parents dragged me along to a dinner party at Asha Patel's house. My brother was at a sleepover. I had begged for a babysitter so I could stay home, preferably sixteen-year-old Lonnie Marshall from next door, who was so totally gorgeous, but my parents had not acquiesced. Asha and I were the same age. So Asha and I would hang out in one room while the adults hung out in another. Great. Asha was the most boring girl alive.

The night didn't start out so bad because I discovered Asha's parents had rented *The Exorcist* to view over the weekend. Ignoring Asha's protests that it wasn't a proper movie for kids, I turned off the lights and began watching.

Halfway through I had to hit pause because Asha was practically hyperventilating with fright and swearing that the Devil had made the olives in her pizza turn into cockroaches. I decided to take a break anyway and go downstairs for a Coke.

The adults were all sitting around the fire, talking and having drinks. Grabbing a can I went unnoticed and prepared to leave when I heard my name mentioned.

"Maya?" my dad laughed. "Not likely."

"No really," Mr. Patel said. "Asha just wrote an essay and submitted her grades. There are still a few openings left at the school."

"Maya isn't interested in math and science," my mom replied. "She likes movies and those Sweet Valley High books."

My dad shook his head. "Complete waste of time. Useless. Now Samir is showing quite a bit of potential. In a few years, maybe he can apply there?"

Mr. Patel took a sip of his drink. "Asha's looking forward to it."

"Asha is a special girl." My mom smiled.

My dad sighed. "I only wish Maya were more like her."

Standing in the dark, the moisture from the Coke can wetting my hand, I felt a tremendous ache in my chest, like I couldn't breathe. Finally, I turned, ran into the bathroom, shut the door, and began crying.

I never said a word to my parents.

I managed to convince myself that I didn't care, that it didn't bother me that my parents thought I had no potential.

I might not have said a word, but I didn't need to. I had lived up to their image of me. And I would still be living it, pretending I didn't care, if Ram and Sanjay hadn't jumped me at LAX.

I grabbed a tissue from the box on my bedside table and wiped my face dry.

Seriously, my emotions were in a frenetic flux. One moment I was cool, the next I was crying. I was in a state of perpetual PMS.

Breathe.

Tomorrow was another day. I would try my best. I would take all of this more seriously. I would learn to kick malignant ass. I would do a good job.

I would be the Goddess of Destruction.

As I drifted off to sleep, a little voice reminded me of another responsibility. I would have to tell my parents the truth about Tahir—that we were completely uninterested in each other and would never marry.

I shoved that voice into a deep hole.

One thing at a time.

Chapter 18

"BLOODY HELL, you drive like a whirling dervish on PCP."

I gritted my teeth and eased up on the gas. Tahir was the absolute king of backseat drivers. Maybe on the way back we'd stop off at a secluded cliff, I'd lure him near the edge, summon up another gale-force wind, and wave good-bye as he was blown over. Sounded like a plan to me.

"I'll drive on the way back," he said.

"No way! Here we drive on the right. Besides, there aren't any cows or elephants on the road, and I'm afraid you'll be confused." It was a low blow, but I smiled as I watched his jaw tighten.

"I'll have you know I did my MBA at Wharton, where I drove regularly in Philadelphia traffic for two years."

"Oh really, was that on your bio data? Somehow I missed it," I said sweetly.

"And where exactly did you attend college? Some party school no doubt."

"You're such a snob!"

"You're the one who implied elephants and cows clog the roads in India," he pointed out.

"Don't they?"

He sighed. "Yes."

"Well you were right about the party school," I admitted. "UC Santa Barbara."

"Stunning location."

I smiled. "Definitely."

Our destination now appeared before us, composed of sparkling fountains, sidewalk carts, ocean breezes, and tree-lined, Spanish-tiled walkways.

Fashion Island.

Loyal customers of the locale referred to the site as Newport Beach's premier outdoor shopping experience. Never, ever, to be confused with anything so bourgeois as a mall.

It was still early, barely ten, but almost all the spots directly in front of the entrance were full. As it turned out there was one slot at the end, but I drove past it. Too tight a squeeze.

"You just passed a spot," Tahir pointed out.

"It was too small."

"No it wasn't."

"Yes it was. Trust me."

"I don't. You could easily have done it."

After three more aisles of arguing, I pulled in front of the spot, got out, and chucked Tahir the keys, hard. He caught them easily, jumped in the driver's seat, backed up, angled the H2 to the right, and slid into the spot perfectly, with room to spare.

He hopped out, oozing with satisfaction, and tossed me back the keys. I reached out to catch them and missed. I snatched the keys from the pavement, snagging a nail in the process and stalked past Tahir.

I could control the forces of nature, but apparently I couldn't park.

I sped up, but Tahir kept up the pace easily, and had the nerve to whistle. Dammit, he even did that well!

"I don't know," Tahir mused, coming out of the dressing room. "I like the gray pinstripe better."

"They all look amazing on you," the salesman said, rushing forward.

Like a magnet, Tahir's ass called to me. I spent a good moment appreciating its merits. Honestly, did he spend half his day doing butt-tightening exercises or what? I managed to tear my gaze away, but the Neiman Marcus salesman to my left had no such self-control. He was openly gawking.

Tahir was unfazed by the man's attention; he was too busy checking out his image in the mirror. I couldn't conceal a sigh of impatience. As much as I lived and breathed shopping, Tahir was rapidly turning me off my favorite sport. He was able to detect minute differences in the exact same pieces of apparel.

He raised an eyebrow in my direction. "What do you think?"

"The pinstripe," I said for the fourth time.

"Hmm." He turned back to the mirror.

From the deep reaches of my purse, a Louis Vuitton monogrammed minibag, the James Bond theme song erupted. I looked around to see if anyone dared mock my choice of ringing tone and pulled out my cell phone. I flipped it open. "Hello?"

"This is Ram!"

The sheer loudness of his voice had me clamp my hand to my ear, and hold the phone six inches away from my head. Very, very cautiously, I removed my hand but kept the phone at a safe distance.

"Hey, Ram. You're not calling halfway around the world, you know. You don't have to shout."

"Of course I'm not calling that far!" he shouted.

It was a lost cause. "What's goin' on?"

"I am talking to you, that is what is going on. Where are you?"

"Fashion Island. I'm showing someone around."

"You should be vanquishing evil."

I rolled my eyes. "I had a little encounter last night."

"Oh? How did it go?"

"Not very well."

"Hence your need for practice."

I looked over at Tahir, and he quickly turned his attention back to the mirror. I'd swear he'd been listening in, though. I dropped my voice to a whisper. "I'm in the best place for that, Ram. There are people all around me. If the good, the bad, and the ugly show up, my Malevolent Meter will know."

There was a long pause, then Ram said, "Are you ready for your next lesson?"

Ready? When had I been ready for any of this?

I looked up and sure enough, Tahir's reflection stared back at me from the mirror. I couldn't tell if he was eavesdropping or just staring. I moved off a few feet and turned away for good measure. "Okay," I said into the phone. "I'm ready. When and where?"

"Tonight."

Tonight was Aunt Gayatri's party. Okay, now I had two things to weigh. On one hand, strengthening my powers so I could one day restore the balance of good and evil in the world. On the other, facing the onslaught of familial wrath, maternal silent treatment, and internal guilt if I dared not attend.

The world would have to wait, just for a few hours.

"Not tonight," I said. "Tomorrow? I can be there as early as you want," I threw in helpfully.

"I do not rise before afternoon," Ram said.

"Jet lag?"

"No, I prefer to sleep late."

"I thought holy men were supposed to wake at dawn and bathe in mountain springs or something," I said.

"I cannot think of anything more intolerable," Ram replied. "We will meet tomorrow at one, in time for lunch. I have heard of another great place."

Visions of Burger King danced in my head. "How about if I choose the restaurant?"

"Then it is so." He hung up.

I turned around and my nose came squarely in contact with Tahir's solid chest. "Ow!" I said, but stayed there a moment longer. Very, very solid.

"Who's Ram?" he asked.

"A man who worships the ground I walk on." Well it was true, in a way.

"The poor lad must not get out much." Tahir walked away, a Neiman Marcus bag in each hand.

Oh yeah, the guy was definitely going down.

Chapter 19

I REQUESTED the patio.

The food at Las Brisas was good, but the view was absolutely delicious. I didn't know if it was that, or the dirty martini with extra vodka, but as soon as our appetizers were served, the mood had settled into one of almost semipleasantness.

Ocean breezes seemed to have a positive effect on Tahir. He was sitting back in his chair, relaxed, sipping on a glass of Chardonnay, and staring out at the Pacific. He hadn't said one irritating thing since we'd left Fashion Island; in fact, he'd been rather silent.

I hated to spoil the mood, but it was time we had a talk. "There's something we need to discuss."

He continued to stare out at the view. "I'm not telling your parents."

"Why?" I demanded. "I can't tell them! I'm already the black sheep of the family. You want me to go down to mutton? Just say you're not interested."

Finally, he turned toward me. "Tell the people who

are currently hosting me that I have no interest in their one and only daughter? That would be unbelievably rude." He set his wineglass down and took a bite of his scallops. "Lovely."

My ahi salad remained untouched. "You don't want to be rude? You've been nothing but since you arrived."

He took another bite and looked at me coolly. "And how exactly would you describe someone who leaves another stranded at the airport?"

Touché. "I had my reasons."

He rolled his eyes. "Ah yes, the neo-Nazis."

"White supremacists."

"May I try your ahi?"

I was about to refuse, but that would be *rude*. I pushed over my plate.

"Why aren't you married?" he asked, helping himself to a rather large portion of my salad. "How old are you? Thirty-one, thirty-two?"

I snatched the plate back. "I just turned thirty, which is still young. Besides, I get carded all the time at bars."

He smirked. "There must be a rash of legally blind bartenders in the state."

My eyes narrowed. "God, you're such an asshole."

"Most women find me irresistible."

"Just to clarify, we're talking about women brainwashed by society, victimized by double standards, who also possess low self-esteem?"

To my surprise, he laughed.

His laugh was more mouthwatering than the ahi.

Even white teeth, the slender yet strong line of his neck, the way his eyes lit up . . .

He reached for my plate again, but I swatted at his hand. "Hand over the scallops, and you've got a deal." He did. The mood at the table returned to one of semi-semipleasantness.

Then—

"Why don't you have a job?" he said.

I do. Fighting evil.

I wanted to tell the truth. I wanted to tell everyone. I couldn't, for two reasons.

Growing up in an Indian family, it becomes second nature to hide everything from your parents. First it was makeup, then non-Indian boyfriends, now bottles of Grey Goose vodka and, of course, my true dharma.

Secondly, what would I say? I'm Kali reborn, but last night I got my ass kicked by two thugs at a convenience store.

The time wasn't right. Not yet.

Seriously, though, the guy wasn't the most stimulating of conversationalists. He had brought up my age, my unmarried and unemployed status. What would he bring up next, my unfertilized eggs? On the subject of raising kids, I'd rather save the Universe . . . twice. Without doubt, it would be easier.

Instead of answering his question, I took a sip of my drink.

Tahir polished off the ahi. "You're incredibly spoiled, you know that?" He eyed my scallops.

Like I was going to share after that comment!

I pulled the plate closer toward me. "Look who's talking! How many servants does your family employ back in Delhi?"

He shrugged. "There happens to be an excess of labor in the country."

"And my parents happen to have more money than Solomon, malpractice insurance aside." I speared a scallop with force. "And what exactly do you do? You said something about moving here permanently." Maybe I could report him to the INS?

"Ah yes, I did mention that to you before you left me stranded at the air—"

"Just to clarify," I interrupted. "How long are you going to keep throwing that in my face?"

He smiled. "A while, do you mind?"

His smile caused the scallop to lodge in my throat. I took a gulp of water. "You were saying . . ."

"I was vice president of International Acquisitions at Metro Bank in Delhi. When the position of senior manager of the Asia Division at the Los Angeles office came my way, I jumped at it. It's quite a step up."

"How interesting," I said without interest. "Now if you don't mind, I'm going to the ladies' room." I rose delicately, smoothing my skirt.

Tahir held up his empty wineglass. "If you see the waiter on the way to the toilet, send him over."

My lips in a thin line, I spun on one heel. The waiter was right in my path near the door, so I reluctantly relayed the message, and looked back in time to see Tahir set my plate of scallops in front of him.

Environmentally conscious, I used just one paper towel to dry my hands. A dab or two of matte face powder, a smear of lip gloss, and I was ready. I breezed through the restroom door. Maybe after dropping off Tahir, I'd cruise around, see if my Malevolent Meter went—

Ugh!

I gasped and placed a hand over my middle.

Malevolence. Close by.

My eyes zoomed past waiters, waitresses, busboys, customers—and widened in disbelief.

Wickedness wore a powder blue Chanel suit.

She was slender, middle-aged, well coiffed, with cornflower blue eyes and honey gold hair. Elegant, expensive pearls lined her wrists and throat. Her most striking accessory, though, had to be the cloud of evil that rose off her like a foul-smelling perfume.

She thanked the waiter by name.

"You're always welcome, Mrs. Danner," he said gallantly and with a fawning bow.

Danner? My mind raced. Gwen Danner?

And then it came to me. All those mornings spent happily wading through the society pages, having tossed aside the Current Events section, using Business or Op-Ed as a coaster for my glass, I read about the doings and undoings of Orange County's richest.

Gwen was the creamiest of the creme de la creme of

Newport Beach, one of many tennis-playing, black-and-white ball-attending, socialite-philanthropists who lined the Pacific Coast.

And she was gone.

Racing out the door and to the parking lot, I spied her getting into a blue Jaguar the exact color of her suit. She handed the valet a twenty. Obviously, generous tipping and evil doing weren't mutually exclusive.

I ran to the valet and handed him my ticket. "Please hurry." He slowly walked off. Okay, now he'd be lucky if I threw my spare change at him.

Precious minutes later I was tearing out of the parking lot, scanning the street for the Jag. Finally, I saw it, four cars ahead.

I wasn't sure what I was supposed to do. I only knew I couldn't fail. Not again.

As I zoomed after Gwen, I remembered Tahir at the table waiting. He would not be happy being stranded again. Actually this time he would be significantly unhappier.

I'd left him with the bill.

Chapter 20

GATED ENTRANCE. High walls. Armed guards. Maximum security.

Welcome to Camino Real, the most exclusive country club in Orange County.

From a safe distance I watched the guard wave Gwen's Jag in. I wondered what she was doing there, stopping by for a round of golf? I quickly discarded the thought. It wouldn't make sense if I were supposed to wait two hours, two days, or two weeks for Gwen Danner to do something evil. The Universe was more efficient than that.

Something was going to happen soon.

Gwen wasn't there to lob tennis balls with the tennis pro or issue rude demands to the help.

She was there to do something very, very bad.

And I had a feeling it was far worse than pouring old mayonnaise into the shrimp salad.

I drove slowly up to the gate. I was about to call the goddess but the guard looked like your average man.

Maybe a heady dose of beauty and charm would convince him to let me in.

Fifteen minutes later I was still at the gate, having giggled, flirted, and cajoled to the best of my ability. The guard continued to stand there, arms folded, offering nothing.

I lowered my Gucci sunglasses and widened my dark brown eyes at him. "Honestly, do I look like someone who would try to sneak into a country club? I have better things to do. Gwen Danner really is expecting me."

He continued to stand there, unmoving.

I threw up my hands. "For God's sake I drive one of the most expensive cars on the market!"

"Yeah," he said. Then reached out and gently caressed the fender.

"Listen." I rummaged through my purse until I came in contact with the slim silver card case. "Here's my card. Anytime you want to drive it, you can, and I'm not talking customary humdrum test drive. You can burn rubber—but only if you let me in."

He took the card. "How 'bout now?"

"No. There's no time. It's an emergency."

"Gwen Danner's invitation to the ball get lost in the mail?"

I sighed. "Something like that."

He hit the remote and the gates swung open. "Go on in. And I'll be calling for that ride." He grinned. Wouldn't want to miss another opportunity to stroke your fender."

Ha. Ha. Double entendre. I get it.

I wasn't about to lay down my dating rules right then and there. "Thanks," I called out, and hit the gas.

I was speeding so fast up the long, cemented drive I barely noticed the exquisite grounds.

Okay, maybe I noticed.

I hated country clubs. I despised their homogeneous membership, their backward, narrow-minded thinking, and their superior air.

But mostly I resented not being a member.

My parents were in the upper tax bracket but didn't exactly hang with the "right" crowd.

Personally I didn't mind restrictions, provided I was the one doing the restricting.

I parked and ran to the entrance, rather difficult in my Bruno Magli slingbacks, and stopped outside.

I wouldn't make the same mistake I did at the convenience store.

No way was I taking one step inside without calling the Goddess Within.

I closed my eyes and took a deep breath.

Lightning split the sky.

Chapter 21

NO AURAS. No gale-force winds.

Ram was right. Only what I chose to happen . . . happened. It was as if some part of me *knew* exactly what to do.

I guess you could call it divine protocol.

I was filled with confidence, brimming with energy. There wasn't a doubt in my mind I would stop Gwen. The "how" and "why" were still unclear, but that was irrelevant. Once again I was that little girl jumping off the roof, knowing I would be safe, knowing I could do anything.

I swept into the club foyer and looked around.

The dining room was to my left. Gwen was in there. I could feel her.

The maître d' blocked my path as I reached the door. "Members only."

I held his gaze. "Are you sure about that?"

He paused, then swept his arm out. "Welcome, madam."

Holy Jedi mind tricks, Batman!

I stepped into the room.

Gwen Danner was seated at a small dais in the back of the room, a Coach tote at her elbow. The bag was to die for—

Literally.

Gwen was packing a small machine gun inside.

It wasn't like I had X-ray vision or anything. When I looked at the bag a picture formed in my mind, and I knew what was inside. I wasn't about to volunteer my services for airport security, though.

Not when Gwen Danner, socialite extraordinaire, was about to star in *Country Club Carnage*.

I remained in position, waiting. The time wasn't right. Not yet.

A distinguished, steel-haired man moved to the podium. "Ladies and gentlemen, please give a round of applause for our new club president, Abby Michaels."

A petite silver-haired woman stood.

So did Gwen.

I stepped forward but continued to wait. No one else in the room seemed to notice anything odd—maybe they thought Gwen was heading for the restroom.

"I want to thank those of you who voted for me," Abby said softly into the microphone. "Being club president is a dream come true, I—"

"I'm the rightful president, you bitch!" Gwen screamed, and pulled the machine gun out of her bag. The entire room went still. Abby's face drained white.

I had to admit, the machine gun went pretty well with the pearls and the suit.

I moved forward. "Not so fast, Gwen."

Maybe it was the distance, maybe Gwen's emotions were too strong, but she refused to be swayed by my Goddess Gaze. "You're not a member!" she spat.

I put my hand on the shoulder of a woman at the table next to me. She looked up. "Call the police," I said.

"Don't you dare, Joanna," Gwen warned.

The woman looked back at me. "It's okay," I said. She nodded and began dialing.

I was now in front of the dais. My brown eyes trained on Gwen's blue. "Put the gun down, now."

She responded by opening fire.

Okay, so I really needed to try something other than the Goddess Gaze.

I wasn't about to test my supposed miraculous healing powers by acting like a human shield and dived to the ground. Besides, bullet holes would wreak havoc with my new Bebe shirt.

Gwennie was seriously pissing me off.

She reached into her tote and pulled out another clip.

I raced forward, dived over the dais, and threw myself in front of Abby, knocking her down.

"Everyone get down!" I yelled. Why they hadn't earlier was beyond me.

Thankfully, everyone listened and I had a roomful of rich people kissing the floor. Gwen started shooting, tearing up the walls, paintings, and chandeliers.

I tackled her at the knees. She didn't let go of the gun and continued shooting straight up. Pieces of ceiling began to rain down on both of us. Plaster was not a good look for me, and I grabbed the gun, flinging it aside.

Gwen knew how to fight like a girl, too, and lunged, a mass of bared teeth and French-manicured nails. I clipped her on the side of the head, and she was down for the count.

My heart was pounding.

Blood roared through my veins.

Goddamn I felt great.

I stood up and faced the room. I was tempted to throw out my arms and shout, "Bow before me, mere mortals," but Abby Michaels was coming toward me.

"Gwen didn't like losing the election," she said shakily.

"No shit."

An older gentleman came and put a protective arm around Abby. "I think this calls for rescinding Gwen's membership, don't you?"

"The police have arrived," someone called out.

The fuzz hadn't responded nearly this fast to the convenience store robbery. Ali would not be surprised.

Time to leave.

I spied a back entrance and quickly headed toward it.

"Wait," Abby called. "We don't even know your name."

I turned and flashed a smile. "Call me the goddess."

And then I was out the door and running toward the parking lot.

*   *   *

The same guard opened the gate. "The police are here, what's going on?"

I met his gaze. "You won't remember me."

He nodded. "I won't remember you."

I sped away, then stopped, and reversed. "Ah, can I have my card back." It had my name and phone number on it, which sort of defeated the purpose of the mind control thing.

Silently, he handed me the card.

I was off, feeling great and ready for some more action.

I turned on the radio. Instead of my favorite hip hop station, I moved the dial to local news.

I didn't have to wait very long.

Gang members involved in a Compton shoot-out had broken into a home, and were holding the entire family hostage.

I'd been heading home but made a U-turn, toward the 405 North and Los Angeles. The excitement began building inside me.

I was going to save this family.

I was going to pound some ass.

I was Maya Mehra, Goddess of Destruction.

I'd be bigger than the Taj Mahal.

Chapter 22

I WAS LATE to Aunt Gayatri's dinner party.

A taboo on the same level as eating a cow . . . not that I worshipped cows, but I did meet a chick from Minnesota who did, and she wasn't even Hindu.

The party was in full swing.

Across the room my mom was shooting me looks cold enough to make my teeth hurt. But I didn't care. I'd just defeated a crazed machine-gun-wielding socialite. I would have taken on the gang members in Compton, too, if they hadn't surrendered before I got there.

Still, I was feeling pretty good.

The hired bartender handed me a dirty vodka martini, and I was feeling even better.

There were three things you could count on at an Indian party. One, a fully stocked bar, two, enough catered food to feed an army, and three, Bose speakers blasting the latest Bollywood hits.

But that didn't make these get-togethers enjoyable.

Call me prejudiced, but I just don't get along with people from my ethnic gene pool.

Most Indian guys are mama's boys who, even after the age of thirty, are still whipping out their SAT scores at parties. Indian chicks are compulsively competitive. They may go to Ivy League schools, dye their hair, and earn their own income, but deep down inside they're all after the same high-scoring SAT boys.

My mom must have grown cross-eyed from shooting me dirty looks because she marched over. "Why aren't you wearing Indian clothes?" she demanded. "That top is see-through."

"It's not see-through, it's Ce-line." I pointed out. "And you know it shows far less flesh than a sari."

"Why did you leave Tahir at the restaurant?" Before I could see if the Goddess Gaze worked on her, she added, "Thank God Nadia was there lunching with a friend. She brought Tahir home."

"Nadia?" I couldn't keep the disgust from creeping into my voice. Well I could, but why the hell should I? I quickly surveyed the room, and, sure enough, Nadia and Tahir were outside on the patio. My eyes narrowed.

Nadia was my cousin, and my mortal enemy, the only other Mehra girl, other than me, who wasn't married. You'd think that would bring us together.

Not.

Nadia was a nephrologist. Whatever that meant. She'd just moved back to Southern California after abruptly leaving New York. Rumors hinted at a failed relationship, but I personally thought it was by mayoral decree.

As I watched, Nadia leaned over and flirtatiously put her hand on Tahir's arm, giggling up at him over the rim of her drink. The embroidered white sari was pretty, but wrapped so tightly around her figure I was surprised she wasn't keeling over in a perpetual faint. Her black hair was cut short in a sleek, shiny bob. In my opinion her eyes were too wide and her lips too small, but I could see how some men would find her attractive—if they fancied a demented ethnic version of Betty Boop.

To my annoyance, Tahir seemed to be enjoying the attention. He was smiling and nodding down at her. My hands closed tightly on the stem of my glass. Because all the guests thought Tahir and I were semiengaged, it was hopelessly disrespectful that Nadia should flirt with him—and he should like it—right under my nose.

"I'll be right back," I said to my mom.

Nadia smiled bitchily as I came through the glass doors and onto the patio. "Well, look who finally arrived."

I responded with a thousand watts of my own bitchiness, and glanced over at Tahir. His expression was unreadable, his face cold. I felt a slight pang of regret; I'd actually started to like the guy.

"Maya's sort of the family pet project." Nadia giggled. "We all keep waiting for her to grow up and find herself."

Ho! She did not just say that!

I toyed with the green olive in my glass. "You know,

Nadia, I heard the most illuminating bit of information the other day. That medical school you supposedly went to in the Caribbean? It's actually a voodoo learning center." My eyes widened. "Gee, I hope the AMA doesn't find out about that."

Tahir cleared his throat. "If you ladies will excuse me." He brushed by me as he left.

"Sure," Nadia smiled, then turned toward me, her eyes hardening. "What the hell's your problem?"

"Oh I'm sorry, did I interrupt a precious moment between you and my semifiancé?"

Nadia sneered. "Oh right, like the two of you are really happening. You dumped him at the restaurant, and from what I hear, it's not the first time."

I downed my drink and set the glass aside. "Just because your life sucks, don't take it out on me."

Nadia pressed a hand to her chest. "My life sucks? I'm not thirty, living off my parents, with no career to speak of, and no friends. I'm a successful nephrologist—"

I interrupted. "What is that actually?"

"It's very complicated. It deals with nephrology." I rolled my eyes, and she continued furious, "I'm twenty-eight. I'm financially independent—"

"Your parents paid for your education, they paid for your apartment in Manhattan, and now they're paying for your condo in Redondo—"

"It's an investment," Nadia snapped.

"And it rhymes." I turned away. For a moment I was struck by a feeling of loneliness so powerful, it nearly brought tears to my eyes. It was true. I didn't have friends. I had shopping buddies. Friendship based on fashion trends and platinum credit. I couldn't imagine telling any one of them what I was going through.

One of my ex-boyfriends, Mark Carter, still lived in the area. He was a good listener, and I'd toyed with the idea of calling him. But then I remembered why we'd broken up. Mark had taken me over to meet his parents and have Sunday dinner with them. The first thing his mother said after meeting me was, "I'm surprised you speak English so well." I didn't dump Mark because of his parents. I dumped him because he didn't correct them.

So Nadia was right. Didn't mean she was getting off the hook though.

I took a shaky breath and tried to get a grip. No one messed with the goddess.

I smiled and turned back to face her. "Look up and watch."

I really only had to close my eyes for a second.

Veins of lightning spread through the cloudless sky.

Nadia's mouth dropped open, and she stared at me.

I stepped as close to her as I could without gagging. "There's more where that came from." Then I tossed my hair and strode back into the house.

Now it was Tahir's turn.

I spied him standing in the center of a group of men, all of whom were visibly sucking in their guts and fingering their wallets. Poor lads, without a doubt Tahir's was still bigger . . .

Before I could head over, though, I heard my name being called. Aunt Gayatri and Aunt Dimple were bearing down on me like two scud missiles on a poorly defended target.

Aunt Gayatri was tall and thin with patrician features. Her long black hair was pulled back in an elegant French twist. She wore a salwaar kameez, composed of a long shirt and loose, flowing pants. Aunt Dimple was wearing a salwaar kameez, too, but instead of flowing, the shirt bunched up around her stomach and hips.

Damn! What did they want?

"Hi." I hugged both my aunts, then aimed what I hoped was a bright smile at Aunt Gayatri. "Thanks for throwing this great party."

Her smile was cool and assessing. "What do you think of Tahir?"

Aunt Dimple grabbed my arm and pressed me to her side. "Oh, Maya loves him, I can already tell. And why shouldn't she? The man is sweeter than an Alphonso mango and twice as juicy."

Eww.

Aunt Gayatri was studying me. "Women who have children before thirty decrease their risk of breast cancer. Since you're past the deadline, I suggest a very short engagement and frequent sexual activity to ensure you become pregnant the first month of marriage. Are you on the pill?"

More eww!

Both my aunts had at least one grandchild apiece and therefore had nothing better to do than focus on my reproductive abilities. I needed the attention off me. "You know Nadia is still single."

Aunt Gayatri would not be distracted. "Nadia is younger than you and has assured me she will be engaged by the end of the year."

I spotted Nadia in a corner, half-listening to the conversation around her, practically undressing Tahir with her eyes.

Not a bad idea . . .

I followed her gaze, and my body temperature rose ten degrees.

"Maya's aroused, I recognize the signs," Aunt Gayatri said in a satisfied voice. "No doubt her inner labia have begun to swell and darken in color."

I mentally replaced Tahir's clothes and found both my aunts watching me with identical expressions of approval.

Aunt Dimple reached up and kissed me on the cheek. "I'll call Tahir's mother to set a date." Her voice dropped to a whisper. "Go turn that mango into a mango shake."

Mortified beyond belief, I watched them walk away.

I continued on my course toward Tahir and laid my hand on his arm. He flinched.

Okay, that was weird.

"Can I talk to you?" He seemed about to say no. "Please," I added.

"Fine."

"Outside?"

He nodded and followed me. I returned to the secluded patio area, but when I turned around he wasn't there. I spied him at the buffet table.

I walked over. "Hey, I thought we were gonna talk?"

He was heaping his plate with tandoori chicken, samosas, and two kinds of chutney, a sweet brown and the one I preferred, a spicy green mint. "Since you're undoubtedly about to embark on a long pathetic excuse of some sort, I thought I'd build up my strength."

"It's not an excuse," I began, but he'd already walked away. Since he was heading in the right direction, I didn't go after him. Instead, I filled my plate up as well. I took quite a few of the samosas, crispy fried dough on the outside and seasoned potato on the inside.

Tahir was sitting on the wall, skillfully balancing his plate and eating. Not a single crumb dared migrate toward his clothes. I sat down next to him. He moved over.

Well, excuse me! Most men would draw swords to be in his position.

"Listen, before we talk about the fact that my aunts are inside planning our upcoming wedding, I want to apologize. I'm sorry I left you at the restaurant today, but I absolutely had no choice. The reason is something I'm not at liberty to discuss right now, but one day I'll tell you. That's a promise."

"I understand." He sounded almost pleasant.

"You do?"

"Of course. I didn't see it before, but now it's quite clear to me. Do you mind, I'll return shortly."

He returned with more food.

I set my plate aside. "What do you mean you didn't see *it* before?"

Tahir chewed thoughtfully on a piece of lamb kebab. "My friend back in Delhi has a sister. Nice girl, but a bit off somehow. Always disappearing for no reason. Coming up with crazy stories that never made much sense. The family took her to a clinic in Switzerland. I hear she's much better now."

I stood up, eyes blazing. "You think I'm crazy?"

Tahir glanced up at me nonplussed. "Aren't you? What else could it be? First the airport, then today at lunch—When I first met you I wondered why a girl who's obviously very pretty would need an aunt to find her a boy. Now it makes sense."

"First of all I never asked my aunt to find me a boy. Second of all, you're single yourself. Does that make you nuts?"

"I'm not single," he corrected. "I'm unavailable. Women have never been a problem."

"Right, because you have so many others."

"You know Nadia made an interesting point. She said you've always been a loner. No one in the family is able to get close to you, not even your brother."

"You're talking to Nadia about me!" I was so angry, I was probably grinding the cosmetic veneers right off my teeth.

Ugh.

The malevolence hit so suddenly I would have fallen if Tahir hadn't reached out and grabbed me. "What is it?" he demanded.

Evil. Thick and cloying, wrapped around me, I could barely breathe.

I wanted to stay there, wrapped in Tahir's arms. Trust the guy finally to make contact at the worst possible moment. I looked up. His dark eyes were intent on my face, filled with an emotion I would have liked to explore—

But the malevolence was a living, breathing thing. Seeping in through my nostrils and my mouth. Mingling with the taste of the lamb kebab in a very unappetizing way.

I broke away and made a quick scan of the patio.

Evil-free.

I ran into the house.

Nothing.

This wasn't one of the guests.

This was someone new.

I yanked open the front door. The cul-de-sac was empty. Quiet. Mehra cars lined the circle. My H2 stood out like a bright yellow beacon in a sea of subdued Mercedes-Benzes.

I walked into the middle of the street.

By the time I heard the car engine it was too late.

Chapter 23

YOU WOULD THINK that a goddess could just point, click, and send the car off to another realm, or at least New Jersey.

As it was, the black car came zooming at me so fast, I barely had time to fling myself to the side.

The hot air from the exhaust washed over me as the tires screeched to a halt. The door opened, and a male voice hissed, "The personification of evil on Earth must die."

Was he talking about *moi*?

Before I could get a good look at the driver, the lights from an oncoming car blinded me with their brightness.

Once again I was in the path of an oncoming car.

I shuffled on my belly and managed to move a few inches.

The car missed me . . . barely.

The driver of the first car sped off.

There I was in the gutter. My clothes torn, Prada shoes scratched beyond repair, my kidneys bruised and damaged. Okay, the last bit was a guess, but if anything had happened to my kidneys, it wasn't like Nadia was going to give me one of hers.

Shakily I stood.

The second car parked, and an Indian family spilled out, heading for Aunt Gayatri's, blissfully unaware they'd nearly done in one of the guests of honor.

I found my purse on the street. A few of the younger guests were outside now; they looked at me curiously, but continued with their conversation. No one ventured to ask if I needed assistance.

We really were the apathetic generation.

Hobbling on my broken heel to the car, I unlocked the door and managed to heave myself into the seat.

I called Ram.

"Hello?" he shouted.

I winced and closed my eyes. "I was attacked, outside my aunt's house. Someone wants me dead." I choked up on the last few words. "He said I was evil and tried to run me over, then I was nearly run over by another car, but that was unintentional."

After a long pause, Ram said quietly, "I was afraid this would happen."

"What?" The lump dissolved in an instant.

"Kali is an oft-misunderstood deity. There are those who believe her to be evil. Naturally they will want to obliterate her human incarnate on Earth."

"Naturally." I leaned my head against the seat. "So this guy sees me as the Antichrist's Indian cousin?"

"Indeed. Although frankly, I did not expect them to find you so quickly, though it stands to reason—if I were able to discover your whereabouts—"

The words exploded from my mouth. "Why? Did you leave a trail of bread crumbs or something?"

"The *how* is irrelevant at this point. Maya, you must not be so careless with your life. You must be on guard at all times against your enemies. Then and only then will you be able to restore the balance of the Earth."

Great. Not only did I have Nadia to contend with, but a fanatical Kali-hater. I couldn't decide who was worse.

Okay, the Kali-hater was worse.

But Nadia was still a bitch.

Chapter 24

BY THE NEXT MORNING I was as fresh as a woman in a feminine hygiene commercial.

The night before, Ram urged me to go home and rest. We would meet for lunch at one as planned. He was quite certain I would not be attacked again. I wasn't so sure, but the comforting lights of the Brinks Alarm System eventually soothed me to sleep. By the time I came downstairs searching for something to eat, it was almost eleven.

My mom was sitting at the counter having a cup of tea. God forbid a tea bag should ever enter the house. The only loose tea permitted was a Golden Orange Pekoe Darjeeling from India, although I knew for a fact she mixed it with Lipton Green Label for body.

I began rummaging through the fridge, and leaned forward to grab a box of mini chocolate donuts.

"Maya, we never finished our discussion from last night. You've been acting very odd lately, and I don't like it."

I grabbed the donuts and straightened too soon, my head slamming into the top of the fridge.

Luckily I was a divinely fast healer.

My mom's face wore its familiar pinched expression. "You're never home, and you never spend any time with Tahir."

Struggling to suppress a groan, I joined her at the table and shoved a donut in my mouth. Politeness dictated I not speak while chewing, and I used the time to think. How dumb was I to think my abrupt disappearance from the airport, as well as my abrupt disappearance from the restaurant yesterday, would be forgotten? My abrupt disappearance from the party last night—certain to come up—was something I was not ready to tackle.

Swallowing pure chocolate goodness, I called up the energy and leveled the Goddess Gaze at my mom. "You will relax. You will not fret over my unmarried status. Your qualms concerning your lack of grandchildren will disappear. From now on your biggest worry will be whether or not the Anna Nicole show is around for another season."

"What are you talking about? Who is this Anna person?" My mom's face went from pinched to puzzled.

Damn, it didn't work!

What the hell was the point of being a goddess if I couldn't get my own mother to do what I wanted?

I looked away and focused the Goddess Gaze on the package of donuts.

"Did you know Tahir is spending the day with Nadia instead of you?"

"Nadia? How did that happen?"

Her face softened. Obviously she mistook my surprise for jealousy. "Nadia called and spoke with Tahir. They're going apartment hunting in LA. Apparently she knows a broker."

"Isn't it a little soon for apartment hunting? He just arrived."

"Metro Bank wants him to start ASAP. Their headquarters are on Wilshire, so Tahir needs a place in West LA."

LA . . . Compton . . . Camino Real . . .

"Where's today's paper?" I demanded.

"Right in front of you," she said calmly, sipping her tea.

"Oh." I grabbed the Orange County edition of the *LA Times*. The article jumped out at me from the bottom corner of the front page. I began skimming. Gwen Danner, yada, yada, yada, prominent socialite, blah, blah, blah, murderous rampage, yak, yak, yak.

Then—

According to Camino Real guard, Ken Burke, a mysterious young woman entered and exited the premises. The description of the woman matched that given by club members as the one who disarmed Gwen Danner. Burke was unable to give a description of the car, except to say that it had nice fenders. Police are seeking the woman for questioning.

I knew Burke had fancied my fenders.

But why had the mind control worked on Burke and not on Gwen or my mother? Ram had some explaining to do. Still, I was thankful. Getting mixed up with the police was not a good idea. Newport Beach was not Gotham, and I was not on a one-on-one basis with the commissioner.

I shoved the chair back.

My mom narrowed her eyes at me over the rim of the teacup. "Where are you going?"

"Errands," I said vaguely.

Tahir and Nadia.

Fervent Kali-haters.

Stupid. Unreliable. Goddess powers.

The day was seriously sucking.

Chapter 25

RAM WAS CARRYING a long, slim package wrapped in brown paper, which he placed on the backseat, and refused to comment on.

I took him to the California Pizza Kitchen since they offered a truly excellent vegetarian pizza. My personal favorite was the barbecue chicken. Ram nearly had a very unspiritual fit when he found CPK only served Pepsi. Thankfully the food calmed him down.

Afterward I drove to the same stretch of beach in Corona del Mar. Ram said we needed to be in an isolated setting.

It was a cold January day, which meant I had to wear a thin sweater over my shirt, and jeans instead of shorts. A true Southern Californian, I deeply resented it.

Ram was dressed the same. I wondered whether he had woolen robes dyed orange for when it was chilly. Then again, cold in Calcutta was a sweltering eighty degrees.

I watched as he ran toward the water, radiating delight. In a moment we'd be having a serious discussion about the unending battle between good and evil. My mentor was an interesting mix of childlike enthusiasm and innate wisdom. Maybe the two went hand in hand?

Wait . . . mentor?

I sat down on one of the rocks. Ram was scouring the beach for shells. I'd definitely grown dependent on the man, not a wise move considering he only had a six-month visa.

Shells gathered in the folds of his robes, he came over to sit by me. "Beautiful, no?"

I picked up a black mollusk shell inlaid with shiny translucent material. "They'll make a nice souvenir."

"No," Ram said. "I will return them to their rightful place. Away from the ocean they will only dry and lose their luster." We sat there quietly for a few moments. "You are troubled."

"Yeah, well, discovering some nut job's out there trying to kill you will do that."

Ram nodded his head. "Yes, that is a problem. However I think something else is weighing on your mind."

Ram was far too shrewd, and I looked away. What was it Nadia had said to Tahir last night? Maya's not close to anyone.

I was tempted to put my head on Ram's shoulder and spill my guts, starting with my childhood.

Come on, Maya.

First of all, Ram's shoulder looked pretty bony, and I'd

probably end up with a crick in my neck. Secondly, when did I ever give a damn what anyone thought?

That little voice inside me was trying to say something, but I pushed her back into the hole and added a shovel or two of extra dirt for good measure.

Besides, this wasn't the time for psychoanalysis, my life sort of hung in the balance. Oh yeah, and the future of the planet, too.

"You weren't surprised to find out someone was trying to kill me. Why?" I said.

"In Hinduism we believe that for everything there is an equal opposite. You are the personification of good, so it stands to reason you will be confronted by the personification of evil."

"That's dumb."

Ram rubbed his chin thoughtfully. "No coin can exist with just one side. The shade cannot exist without the sun."

"But—"

"You like the shade, do you not?" Ram interrupted.

"Of course."

"Exactly." He smiled smugly. "We enjoy the shade, yet continually complain about the sun. Accepting both is the secret to true happiness."

I raised an eyebrow. "Sort of like accepting Pepsi when Coke isn't on the menu?"

Ram frowned. "That is quite different."

"How?"

His frown deepened. "We are wasting time. We must

proceed to the next lesson. Do you recall the story of Kali's creation?"

"I didn't get that far."

"Before the dawn of man, a massive war between the divine and antidivine forces erupted. On the divine side were Shiva, Vishnu, and Brahma—the holy Hindu trinity. On the antidivine side were Raktabija and his band of fellow demons.

"Now try as they might, the holy trinity could not defeat Raktabija. For as soon as one drop of his blood hit the ground, another demon sprang from the spot. Each new demon also had the power to generate more demons from its own blood. Raktabija seemed invincible."

"Speaking of Hindu gods," I mused, "aren't there any human incarnates of Shiva or Vishnu? What about Zeus or Thor? I was thinking we could all go to that new martini bar in Pasadena one night."

Ram cleared his throat. "Shiva, Vishnu, and Brahma decided to combine their powers. The three shot forth piercing beams of light, and at the point of contact, the form of a woman took shape. Forged of light, she was known as the shining one. The goddess was born."

"Typical men," I scoffed. "Sending in a woman to clean up their mess. So then what happened?"

"Kali began by grabbing each demon and devouring it on sight. Not a drop of blood spilled, not an ounce of flesh spared. It was a brilliant plan, she eliminated every demon save Raktabija."

I rubbed my stomach. "Was Kali fat?"

Ram ignored the question. "The goddess and the Demon King began circling each other. Raktabija had a mighty magical mace that emitted fiery sparks as he swung it about, but Kali had no weapons."

"Right, she just ate her way to the top."

Ram removed his glasses and began polishing the lenses with the end of his orange robe. "No, she used her powers to manifest a magnificent ruby-encrusted sword. Raising it high above her head, she released a blood-curdling cry and rushed at the demon."

"A ruby-encrusted sword, huh? Not too shabby. I think I have just the shoes to go with that."

"The battle between the two waged on, but in the end, with a massive strike of her sword, Kali decapitated Raktabija. Thereby releasing his soul from its evil-natured body and mind."

"Great story, Ram, but there's only one problem."

"Yes?"

"I don't have a sword like that. Where could I get one?"

"You do not get one. Now we come to the next lesson."

"Which is?"

Ram hopped off the rock. "You learn how to use this." He picked up the mysterious package he'd carried to the sand, and handed it to me.

I tore away the brown wrapper and gasped. The rubies on the handle gleamed. The shining steel blade was thirty-six inches long.

Kali's sword.

I let out a slow whistle. "Hot damn!"

Chapter 26

"THIS MUST HAVE BEEN a bitch to get through customs." I hefted the sword, letting the remains of the wrapper float down to the sand. "Have the priests of your temple kept watch on this for thousands of years?" My eyes widened. "Like the Lady of the Lake did for Excalibur?"

"What nonsense," Ram scoffed. "The blade was manufactured in Taiwan. The rubies are Burmese. The handle is of my own design," he added proudly. "A swordsmith in Bowbazaar did the assembling." He patted the sides of his robe. "I have the bill here somewhere. If you can just repay . . ."

Tuning him out, I raised the sword above my head and brought it down in a slow, measured sweep. I'd never held anything in my hand that felt more natural.

Despite what an ex-boyfriend had to say.

"This is so fab, Ram! I feel like Duncan in *Highlander*."

"You will practice as I meditate," he said.

"Wait." I lowered the sword to my side and squared

off with him across the sand. "Two things. First, why doesn't my Goddess Gaze work on everyone, and, two, why do I have to keep calling the Goddess Within? Why can't I just stay in that state?"

"You tell me," Ram said.

"You're the expert."

"And you are the goddess," he countered. "Only what you choose to happen—"

"Yeah, yeah, happens, I know."

"You do not. If you truly understood, there would be none of these questions. You believe your powers are temporary; therefore, they are. The essence of strength is belief."

"What if I believe you should bow to me?"

"Do you truly believe I should?"

"No. I'm a Democrat." I kicked at the sand. I was seriously gagging over all this metaphysical stuff. "None of it makes any sense. I mean technically, since I'm a god, shouldn't I be all-powerful? Omniscient, omnipotent, and all the crap in between?"

"Once you fully accept your dharma, everything will make sense, there will be no more questions."

"You know, Ram," I said with a peevish look, "some people say life's a journey. You can't know everything."

He waved his hand. "Buffalo dung. Life is a journey, but all we need to know is inside of us. Just believe. Now, call the Goddess Within."

I did. Lightning instantly slashed across the sky.

Ram looked at me, impressed. "Very good. The sword

you hold in your hands is a powerful weapon, blessed by the priests of my temple. It will serve you well."

"You guys didn't happen to bless any assault weapons or grenades did you? 'Cause those would definitely come in handy."

"You must keep practicing. If you are destroyed, all hope for the world will be lost." He stretched. "In the meantime I will meditate and enjoy this most beautiful ocean." He went back to the rock, took off his wooden sandals, and seated himself in the classic yogic position, eyes closed.

Thirty minutes had passed, and Ram was still deep in a meditative trance.

There was definitely something about the sword. Just holding it made my blood quicken.

I could do amazing things with this sword.

I *knew* I could.

Socialites could keep their machine guns.

However, I was kind of getting bored with the practicing. I had thrust, parried, and swung to the best of my ability. It was actually a pretty good workout, better than Pilates. The goddess workout . . . hmm maybe I could put out my own exercise video like Jane Fonda? Just in case my video game idea didn't take off.

Ram's eyes were open. He was watching me.

I swung the sword around me in a neat semicircle. Yeah, I was showing off, but I felt six feet tall with the thing in my hand.

"Pretty awesome huh?" I grinned. Ram smiled. "Did you have a nice nap?"

"I did not sleep. I was meditating. But yes, I am refreshed."

"So with this sword, am I all-powerful or what?" I asked.

"That is up to you."

"Right." I still thought Ram's theory was wrong.

"We must leave."

"Do you sense something?" I looked around. I didn't feel any malevolence.

"My bowels have fully digested the food," he said with dignity.

"Oh." I put my arm around Ram as we walked back to the car. Suddenly I wanted to do something nice for him. "How about we pick up a case of Classic Coke on the way to Sanjay's?"

His face broke out in a huge smile. "Just the thing I was meditating on."

Chapter 27

ACCORDING TO RAM I didn't have to wait for the Ugh of malevolence to hit.

I could go out looking for it.

He explained this to me as I hefted the carton of Coke all the way up the stairs to Sanjay's apartment. When I asked Ram for help, he pleaded sitar elbow.

Humble servant my ass.

Back in Newport, no one was home—a good thing since the sword would be rather hard to explain, and I didn't want to leave it in the car. My plan was to shower, change, and go back out.

Afterward, dressed in a white silk robe, I threw open the doors of my mirrored, walk-in closet, and with one hand on my chin, the other on my hip, I pondered the eternal existentialist question.

What does a goddess wear to kick ass?

In Style magazine had yet to cover the issue, so it was all up to me. Black seemed a safe bet. I pulled out a black zip-up turtleneck by Guess, my favorite Seven jeans, and black Sergio Rossi slingbacks. Sure, running shoes or Doc Martens would be more appropriate for fighting, but not with these jeans.

I tied my hair back in a bouncy ponytail, added a dusting of Studio Fix powder and some lip gloss, and I was ready. I was going to prove that style and substance overcame malevolence and immorality any day.

I was about to put the divine in *divining* rod.

When I came downstairs I was greeted by the smell of frying onions and garlic.

Mom was home.

I walked into the kitchen to deliver my excuse for the night, but the one busy at the stove wasn't my mom. It was Tahir.

He nodded to the two glasses of red wine on the side table. "Take your pick."

Hmm.

Malevolence was out there, needing to be dealt with.

In front of me was red wine.

A girl needed sustenance.

I took a long, slow sip. "I'm totally loving this Shiraz. Where'd Mom and Dad go?"

"That's obviously Pinot Noir, not Shiraz. We're meeting them at the Kathak show at eight."

"Kathak? They know that stuff bores me to tears. Why'd they buy me a ticket?"

"How can you hate Kathak? The dancers train for decades just to pull off such intricate footwork. It was considered choice entertainment in the court of Mughal emperors."

I responded wittily by sticking my finger down my throat like I was gagging. "So why didn't you go with them? Oh wait—" I batted my eyelashes teasingly. "You wanted to wait for me."

Tahir snorted. "Hardly. I was expecting an important fax; otherwise, I would have joined your parents and their friends for dinner before the show."

I moved closer and peered over his shoulder. "Speaking of dinner, what are you making?"

"Roghan Josh. Lamb curry with potatoes and turnips."

"I know what it is." Honestly, why were people always explaining elementary Indian cultural facts to me?

I was distracted from my irritation by the sight of Tahir's broad, leanly muscled shoulder. No boniness there. I could lean my head for hours and my neck would be fine.

He turned to me. "Are you breathing through your mouth?"

I stepped away, and reached for the wine bottle to fill my glass, which as usual, had miraculously depleted.

Well, I was drinking for two now.

Tahir opened the oven to check on the lamb, and the smell made my stomach roar.

"So what's with cooking dinner?"

He took a sip of wine. "You don't cook, and we both had to eat, so . . ."

Even wearing a ridiculous red apron, Tahir was a splendid specimen of male anatomy. The arm that held the glass of wine up to his Roman nose was powerful yet slender. My limbs melted, remembering the way he'd caught and pressed me to him last night.

Warm fuzzies took up residence in my stomach.

I owed him an explanation for why I'd pulled away and left the party. "About last night—"

He shut the oven door and slung a dish towel over his shoulder. "First of all, you're weird, and not in an appealing way. Second of all, neither of us is interested in a relationship with the other; so let's just agree to lead our own lives without explanation."

The warm fuzzies inside my stomach twisted into gut-wrenching tapeworms. "Fine. But if you think I'm weird, I highly doubt your definition of normal exists."

"Fine," he said.

"Fine."

"You already said that."

"Fine . . . I mean I know." I took a steadying sip of wine. "Are you going to tell my family about us, or do I have to be the sacrificial Sita?"

He removed two plates from the cupboard. "You know this may be a good time for you to tell your family the same thing you told me." His lips curled into a mocking grin. "That you're an independent woman who doesn't believe in arranged marriage."

It was clear now that Tahir was going to be of no help with regard to the marriage mess . . .

I was struck by a strong feeling of déjà vu. Hadn't I had the exact same thought about him before?

I decided to attend the Kathak show, thereby temporarily appeasing my family. Afterward, I'd hit the streets and try to save the world, or at least parts of Orange County.

Until then—

I consented to help Tahir set the table.

Carrying spoons and forks, I tossed them down along with a pile of napkins, buffet style. "So what's with you and Nadia? Is she actually helping you find an apartment?"

Instead of telling me to mind my own business, Tahir began placing the fork and spoon neatly beside each plate and folding the paper napkins into flowers. "And why exactly do you care?"

I picked up one of the tissue tulips and raised an eyebrow. I couldn't decide if the guy was creative or completely anal. "I just feel you should know that Nadia is one warped individual. She doesn't use protective seat covers in public restrooms. She just plops down. I mean that's totally disgusting. And she's a doctor, for God's sake!"

Slipping on bright red oven mitts that matched his apron, Tahir carried over the main dish and a plate of carryout naan he'd warmed in the oven. "And how do you know what she does in a public restroom."

"That's really a long story and not suitable for dinner conversation."

"Speaking of dinner . . ."

We took our seats at the table across from each other.

There wasn't much conversation after that. There we were, two attractive people sharing a delicious meal. It was like a date.

Except I thought he was an asshole, and he thought I was certifiable.

Toward the end of the meal, the fax machine began to beep, and Tahir excused himself from the table.

Leaving the dishes for him, I went upstairs and retrieved my sword.

Grasping the weapon in my hand, I couldn't help smiling.

Who needed a man when I had this?

I'd stash it in the backseat while Tahir was scrubbing away in the kitchen.

Now I was ready.

Chapter 28

IGNORING TAHIR'S BOASTS of parallel parking excellence, *I drove* to the Performing Arts Center in Costa Mesa. After all, this was Orange County. Parking was not an issue. Thousands of acres of orange groves had been paved to make way for parking lots.

Mom and Dad were already in their seats, along with their "friends" Aunt Dimple and Uncle Pradeep.

Honestly, did my parents have any social acquaintances that were not blood-related?

Aunt Dimple started waving as soon as we entered the auditorium and kept it up until we were seated.

It was so totally embarrassing.

There were two empty seats between my aunt and a white guy wearing a T-shirt with the words "I" and "Yoga" separated by a big red heart. Tahir ushered me ahead of him and into the seat next to my aunt.

I had a list of things I'd rather do than watch classical Indian dance, like get my cavities filled without those pesky shots of Novocain or go for a dip in the

Great Salt Lake immediately after a Brazilian bikini wax.

Aunt Dimple kept craning her head to stare at Tahir and me. My mom shot Tahir a warm smile and me a pinched one. My dad was deep in conversation with my uncle Pradeep. I heard the words "HMO" and "referendum" and tuned out.

Bored with what was happening on my left, I turned to my right in time to hear the yoga lover comment to Tahir, "India is such a beautiful and spiritual place. There's this mind-blowing mystical energy, this awesome sense of peace."

"If you ignore all the Hindus and Muslims killing each other," I said.

"Excuse me. I'll be right back." The guy smiled and left.

Tahir shot me a disapproving look. I shrugged, whipped out my cell phone, and began playing games.

By half past eight, the concert still had not started.

Indian standard time.

I don't know whether it was genetics or what, but Indian people were never on time. I'd grown up watching my mom purposely tell all her Indian guests the party started at seven, just so they'd get there at eight—the actual time.

I looked up from the screen to see that Tahir was still staring at me. "What?"

"The show is about to start," he whispered.

"Get a clue." Nevertheless, I put my phone away.

Searching for something else to do, I called the Goddess Within and decided to check out Tahir's aura.

Pulse-pounding red.

I don't know what I'd been expecting. A black aura with horns maybe?

Definitely not scarlet passion, heat, desire . . .

The responding lurch in my body was immediate and powerful, and I forced myself to turn away.

I didn't throw myself at men. I walked over them. Unlike some women—

"Hi, Tahir!"

Nadia stood in the aisle, smiling brightly.

Oozing fake chirpiness, she sat down in the empty seat next to him. "I'm so glad I got a ticket!"

"It's Kathak, not U2," I pointed out. "And someone is sitting there."

Nadia glared at me, then at the yoga guy, who stopped in the aisle and stared confusedly at his seat.

"Hi," he said in a pleasant voice.

"I'm taking your seat," Nadia snapped. She handed him a ticket. "You can have mine."

He took the ticket and folded his hands over it. "Namaste."

Nadia scowled at his retreating back. "Hare Krishna Hippie Freak."

I couldn't keep the disgust from my voice. "God, you're so rude."

Nadia leaned forward. "And you aren't?"

"Ladies." Tahir pushed us back. "The show is starting."

With a final glare at each other we settled into our seats.

"You should be careful," Aunt Dimple whispered in my ear. "I think Nadia is interested in Tahir. Of course," she added, "we'd be happy if either of you ended up with him. He will be quite a good addition to the family."

Wondering what sort of mental defect made me choose to live at home, I slid down into my seat.

The curtains parted.

It was halfway through the show, and I had no clue what was happening on stage.

My Malevolent Meter was also still.

Great, and just when I was looking for a break.

I suppose I could sum up the performance as a lot of intricate hand movements, a lot of heavy ankle bells, and a lot of black eyeliner. Even the solo male dancer had on eyeliner. It made his eye movements appear really exaggerated, which I think was the point.

I knew that the performance tonight revolved around the god Krishna and his soul mate Radha, but that was all. It was too dark to look at my Playbill.

Krishna's mother, obviously hearing rumors of what had happened to the baby Moses over on the next continent, hid her infant son with a childless couple, a goatherd and his wife. Krishna grew up frolicking along the banks of the river with comely fetching gopis or milkmaids. By this time milkmaids and cowherds alike had figured out that Krishna was a god and the human incarnate of Vishnu, the preserver of Hinduism. All the gopis were in love with him, but the one who caught his eye was married, and her name was Radha.

Not to sound blasphemous, but frolicking along the banks of the river with a beautiful married woman might have been okay for Krishna, but around here extramarital affairs get pretty messy. Radha's husband would have lost half his goat herd in California's divorce court.

Around me the audience suddenly held their collective breath. Okay, something was happening.

I really needed to figure out what the big deal was.

I turned to Tahir and saw him wiping at the corner of his eye.

The dude was crying!

I turned back to the stage. I didn't want Tahir to know I had seen him.

Was I an insensitive person? I flashed back to the scene in *Pretty Woman* when Richard Gere took Julia Roberts to the opera. By the end of the performance she's crying, and he's utterly moved by her tears. In her place, I would have fallen asleep, and Richard would have dumped my sorry ass back on the street corner where he'd found me.

I sneaked another peek at Tahir. His eyes were still bright.

Okay, so Krishna and Radha were the ultimate symbol of love.

And yet . . .

In today's time even if true love managed to exist, nagging over money, substandard sex, psychotic sugar-addicted children, vexing in-laws, and work stress would beat it down. Otherwise, why would we have our Dr. Phils and our Judge Judys?

I mean, come on!

The auditorium lights flickered on.

Intermission. Thank God!

I was dying of thirst.

Now, if only I knew how to manifest myself a Cherry Coke . . .

Chapter 29

I'D SWEAR THERE WERE more people in the lobby circling the snack tables than there'd been inside the auditorium watching the show.

Typical Indians.

"That was really, really, really beautiful!" Nadia
squeaked, smiling up at Tahir.

Aunt Dimple was looking at me and inclining her
head toward Tahir.

Super unsubtle.

What was I supposed to do? Push the plates of pako-
das and sweets off one of the snack tables, throw Tahir
down, and have my way with him?

Wisely I settled for a smile. "You really are fond of
Kathak."

"Music and dance move me," he replied.

Tell me about it. I'd seen the tears.

"Such a cultured young man," Aunt Dimple crowed.
"Right, Maya?"

Five pairs of eyes looked from me to Tahir. Mom and

Aunt Dimple shot looks of approval, my dad and uncle shot looks of obliviousness, and Nadia's eyes shot deadly, belladonna-tipped, hemlock-laced, arsenic-sugared darts right at me.

And then—

"This is *her*?" A disbelieving female voice said from behind me.

I turned and was confronted by Ram's cousin Sanjay and a very skinny Indian woman wearing glasses, her black hair scraped back into a tight bun. Her eyebrows curved up in disbelief. "This is *Kali*?"

Crap!

Sanjay quickly got down on one knee, yanking the dubious woman down with him. "Jai Ma Kali! This is my girlfriend, Indira." He paused, and added in a serious tone, "And the battle against the forces of evil, how does it go?"

I shoved back the desire to kick Sanjay in the face and glanced over my shoulder at Tahir and my family. I laughed uncomfortably.

"Did he just call you Kali?" Tahir asked.

"It's a role-playing game, right, Sanjay?" Still on bended knee, Indira beside him, Sanjay stared up at me blankly. "He's Shiva, and I'm Kali."

My dad scratched his cheek. "Shiva? I thought you said his name was Sanjay?"

Aunt Dimple shuddered. "Kali? Why would you want to be her? Sarasvati is the Goddess of Art and Culture— much better and prettier. Some say I look—"

"Excuse me." I yanked Sanjay to his feet and dragged him away. Indira trotted after us, then diverged and headed for the snack table.

When we were at a safe distance, I grabbed him by the front of his shirt. "Who else have you told about this?"

"Just Indira," Sanjay said, puzzled. "But why would you want to hide such glorious news from your family?"

"We have issues," I snapped.

"But Kali-Ma—"

"Just call me Maya, okay?"

"As you wish."

Indira came up sipping a Coke.

Speaking of Cokes . . .

"Where's Ram?" I asked.

"Sanjay and I are on a date. Ram was not invited," Indira said defensively. "Besides, he comes with us everywhere!"

"Now Indu," Sanjay pleaded. "He is my elder and family."

"Don't 'Indu' me!" Indira's eyes blazed. "Bringing him salsa dancing was the last straw! I left India because I was tired of having chaperones on my dates."

"Indira is a chemical engineer," Sanjay bragged.

She scowled. "Don't change the subject."

"But Ind—" he stopped at her look. "Ram stayed at home tonight, didn't he?"

"Only because he wanted to watch *Sex and the City*."

I was about to beat a retreat from their bickering when—

Ugh.

Malevolence at three o'clock.

I spun in that direction—and faced a door marked BACKSTAGE.

A security guard stood at attention.

One of the female dancers ran lightly across the floor, ankle bells tinkling, and the guard stepped aside to let her through.

Ugh.

I was getting past that guard.

This was the distraction I'd been waiting for.

Chapter 30

THE FIRST THING I DID was retrieve my sword from the car.

Tomorrow I was going sheath shopping.

I envisioned black leather with a few silver bells, like the ones the Kathak dancers wore, added to the strap.

It was all about accessorizing.

Then I called the Goddess Within for like the 223rd time that day—although I did love doing it outside. Just so I could see my trademark lightning flash across the sky.

Shazam! There it went.

By the time I returned to the lobby, it was empty. Intermission had ended.

Seeing me, the guard smiled.

Then his eyes fell on the sword.

He reached for the gun in his holster. "Hold on right there!"

The guy was packing a bit much for an Indian dance concert.

Even though it had proved less than reliable, I hit him with the Goddess Gaze. "Let me through . . . just be cool, man . . . relax."

Confucius could not have said it better.

A drowsy smile spread over his face. "Relax." He slumped back against the wall, slowly slid to the floor, and fell asleep.

Huh.

Time to wonder why it happened later. Maybe I'd curl up with a copy of *Metaphysics for Dummies* or something.

Yanking open the door, I stepped through.

The scariest thing backstage was the way the fluorescent lighting mixed with the brown shag carpeting.

I had a nose for wickedness and followed it down the hall. The sounds of pounding feet and music accompanied my footsteps.

The Green Room was empty. So were the dressing rooms. That left only one more place to look.

Would malevolence be waiting in the wings?

Pushing the door open quietly, I stepped into the darkened interior.

Two female dancers slipped offstage, shot me a curious look, and began whispering in a corner. I recognized them as playing two of Krishna's gopis.

Wrongness wrapped around me.

It wasn't coming from the women. I went to the curtain and peered through at the remaining performers on stage.

Nothing.

This was Stanley Kubrick confusing.

"What the hell's going on?" I murmured.

"Shh!" One of the dancers put her finger to her lips.

"Sorry."

"Shh!" the other said.

With the "Shh Sisters" shooting me dirty looks, I inspected every inch of the area, trying to determine the source of malevolence. My search was penetrated by periodic and sharp shh-ing.

Finally, I took a deep breath, closed my eyes, and centered myself.

"Shh!"

Oh come on!

Ignoring everything around me, I tried to focus. A lifelong fan of sugar and high-action Hollywood blockbusters, I was the Queen of Distraction, but I forced myself to concentrate.

The image came to me with Kodak clarity.

Right above my head was a system of pipes . . .

And one of them was leaking.

Gas had accumulated in the ceiling. And just to make things extra exciting, an electrical short circuit was on the way.

I had to get everyone out.

Thanks to the efficient Universe, there was still time.

I opened my eyes.

Malevolence. But not a person. I didn't know I could sense stuff like that. I guess I could now function as a sort of disaster early-warning system for things like gas leaks, earthquakes, the release of a Tom Arnold movie . . .

The two dancers were watching me suspiciously.

"We need to stop the show!" I ran back to the curtain and peered out. How was I going to warn everyone without causing a panic?

One of the dancers grabbed my arm. "Who sent you? Which troupe?"

"What?" She may as well have been speaking HuTu for all I understood. I pulled away and stepped back from the curtain. "Listen, we need to get everyone out. There's a—"

Her foot shot out faster than you could say "impending explosion" and connected with my abdomen. I fell back, still managing to hold on to my sword.

Taking up a graceful stance, the two dancers faced me and waited.

Dancers.

Hence the incredible leg muscles.

With considerably less grace, I stood and decided not to waste time with the Goddess Gaze. It hadn't worked on gun-wielding Gwennie, and I highly doubted it would work on them.

Don't ask me why.

Maybe I'd skip *Metaphysics for Dummies* and go straight to *Metaphysics for Morons*.

Anyway, I didn't want to risk another Kathak kick to my solar plexus.

Time to use my outside voice, as well as my sword.

Grasping the ruby handle, I swung in a warning arc. "Don't mess with me, girls, you won't like the results."

"Our troupe has waited years for an American tour," one of the Shh Sisters said. "We won't let you spoil it."

I stared at them in shock. "There's a gas leak, you dumb shits!"

"Big deal." She sniffed. "Half the concert halls in India have gas leaks."

Okay, enough time wasted. I lunged. Both dancers kicked out together. I stepped aside, protecting my stomach, but it was my right hand they were after. Together their feet came in contact, forcing my hand back, nearly causing me to brain myself with my own weapon. I let go, and the sword went skidding across the floor.

Nice.

So an hour of swordplay on the beach and I wasn't Olympic fencing material. Surprise, surprise.

Weaponless, I contemplated my options.

I'd have to rely on my wits.

I was seriously screwed.

The gopis came at me with another flurry of kicks, which I managed to avoid by running backward like a total dork until I had my back to the wall.

What I needed was pizzazz.

Pure shock and awe.

I centered myself, connected with the warmth, and visualized a familiar fierce wind.

It began with a tickle on the back of my neck.

The breath of a baby breeze.

And then came the roar of its full-grown mother.

Tempest-force gales had chairs, props, and bottles of water flying. The two dancers watched wide-eyed and struggled to gain hold of something. Too late. They fell and were blown onto the stage.

That took care of them.

Feet spread for support; I threw out my arms. "Stop!"

The wind continued to blow.

"Stop! I command—" I lost my balance, fell, and was blown out with the others.

The wind died down and disappeared.

Really nice.

All the dancers were staring at me. The audience was silent.

A voice erupted from the darkness. "Maya! What Are You Doing?"

Mom.

And she was speaking in capital letters.

In the front row a little boy began to cry.

What chain of events, starting from my birth, had led me to be in this position? Facedown on the stage in front of a bewildered audience.

Especially when everyone knew I hated Kathak.

Though now—

I hated destiny more.

Chapter 31

THE LAST CAR had finally left.

My announcement of needing to clear the auditorium because of a gas leak had not been met with panic. Instead, people had shuffled out, grumbling, and demanding their money back. I made a quick call from the lobby phone, since cell phones were traceable, and the appearance of the police, firefighters, and SouthCal Gas Corp. had audience members moving a tad faster.

I didn't wait around after the police arrived. Grabbing my sword, I hightailed it to a secluded vantage point, where I'd wait until the leak had been fixed and everyone safely removed from the premises.

My cell phone rang as flocks of people spilled out into the parking lot.

"How did you know about the gas leak?" my mom demanded.

"I have a sensitive nose."

"Since when? You can't tell the difference between curry powder and talcum powder."

I turned my phone off after that.

One good thing had come out of all this—well, besides all the innocent lives being saved—my abrupt appearance onstage made my previous abrupt disappearances seem positively explainable.

As the last of the fire trucks rumbled away, I headed back to my car. I wasn't worried about someone giving my description to the police. Black hair, brown eyes, tan skin—described about 99 percent of the audience members tonight.

Of course if the words "Aphrodite-like" or "Salma-Hayek-esque" were thrown in—I'd be spotted at fifty yards.

I highly doubted anyone would remember my name from my mom's freaked outburst. If they did, I'd handle it when the time came.

Careening out of the parking lot, I had no intention of going home. I'd keep to the plans I'd made before the concert.

Patrolling time.

Maya Mehra. Goddess of Destruction and Early-Warning Systems.

Not too shabby.

Chapter 32

THE NEXT FEW DAYS took on a routine.

I fought malevolence, avoided my parents, exchanged witty and insulting repartee with Tahir, avoided my parents, consumed mass quantities of Starbucks, avoided my parents, and slept.

This was seriously taking on the drudgery of a job except for one thing.

I wasn't getting paid.

Yeah, there was a lot of variety. Never knowing what form malevolence would take proved interesting. And I wasn't confined to a generic cubicle, spending most of my time in the car driving around. And as a miraculously fast healer, I didn't need expensive health insurance. Of course there was also the added excitement that came from being the target of a fanatic Kali-hater.

Sniper shots as I came out of Starbucks, numerous attempts to run me over, mysterious ticking packages left on the hood of my car . . . I would have actually started fearing for my life if it weren't so obvious the man who wanted me dead had trained extensively in the Inspector Clouseau School of Bumbling Assassins.

I mean seriously, I'd heard the package ticking a mile away. And even if I hadn't, the gigantic red bow on top was probably visible from space.

But with all of the above taking up my time . . .

I never ever got to go shopping!

So coming downstairs late Sunday morning, I wasn't in the most Prozac-y of moods.

I'd spent Saturday night stopping a mugging, stopping a psychotic stalker, stopping a blind date gone bad, and stopping a drive-by shooting. I also stopped a teenager from pushing his grandmother out of the second-story window because she wouldn't give him any more money.

The nice old lady rewarded me with a chocolate chip cookie.

My mood, however, took a significant swan dive from pissy to lethal, when I saw Nadia standing at the bottom of the stairs.

"What the hell are you doing here?" I said politely.

She smirked. "Looks like someone didn't sleep very well. The bags under your eyes wouldn't fit in an overhead compartment."

My face was as smooth and firm as a liposuctioned bottom—a cucumber face mask had seen to that. "As a matter of fact I did have trouble sleeping. What's your excuse? You look positively haggard and fortyish." Before she could reply I noticed the suitcases piled near the door. "What's up with the luggage?"

Nadia shot me a creamy smile. "Didn't Tahir tell you? I found him the most gorgeous apartment in Santa Monica. Now he won't have to stay *here*."

"You're a fast girl, aren't you?" Pun intended.

Nadia didn't get it. "One of my closest friends is in the biz. She pushed through the paperwork. The three of us went to Sky Bar last night to celebrate."

It wasn't fair! They went to Sky Bar, and the highlight of my night was dunking a cookie in a glass of milk.

"You know that weird lightning trick you supposedly pulled the other night?" Nadia asked.

I tossed my hair—I did that a lot. "What about it?"

"I checked the weather report, and there were low clouds in some areas of the Southland. So it was just a coincidence."

"Whatever you want to believe," I said coolly. I had better things to do than convince her I was a goddess. Well, technically, I didn't really have anything to do, but that was beside the point. "Where's Tahir now?"

"The company's set him up with a rental car. As soon as he gets back we're off."

As if waiting for his cue, Tahir came through the front door twirling a set of keys. He was wearing a soft brown V-neck sweater and tan slacks. He looked better than a hunk of Godiva chocolate.

"So you found a place?" I said, establishing my reign as the Duchess of Obvious.

Tahir smiled. "Thanks to Nadia."

I felt an Ugh in my stomach. Not the Ugh of malevolence. More like the Ugh of nausea.

He rubbed his hands together. "Let's be off then. I want to get settled. Starting tomorrow I'm a working man."

"Right." Nadia picked up one of the suitcases and began dragging it toward the door.

"Umm, aren't you going to help her?" I asked him.

"She's doing fine."

"Well, I guess it's good-bye then," I said stiffly, and held out my hand.

Tahir ignored it and turned to Nadia. "Let me give you some help."

She pushed a wisp of hair off her sweaty brow. "Thanks."

"When you stack the luggage, make sure the heavier suitcases remain on the bottom."

"Okay." Huffing and puffing, she managed to open the door with her elbow and haul the suitcase outside.

Tahir returned to facing me. "It never would have worked out between us, you know."

Where did *that* come from?

"What are you talking about?"

He continued as if he hadn't heard me. "I need someone who is proud of her cultural heritage, someone who respects her elders, someone who would make an excellent wife and mother."

Before I could respond he pulled me into his arms and kissed me.

My first thought was—How very unexpected.

My second thought—How dare he!

My third thought—Wait until Nadia sees this!

Then brain activity ceased altogether.

I became pure sensation.

It was as if Cupid had shot an LSD-tipped arrow straight into my heart.

The softness of Tahir's sweater . . . the citrus scent of his cologne . . . each individual muscle in his arms flexing, as he pinned me to him . . . and his mouth . . . soft and controlling, velvety and firm.

I was the shy virginal heroine of a romance novel who suddenly turns wanton at the touch of the hero's mouth.

I was totally begging to be devoured.

Then just when I was hoping he'd use some tongue—

His lips moved to my ear, as his hands slid to my waist and squeezed. "Someone needs to go to the gym."

The Duchess of Obvious had met the Duke of Mood Killers.

I jumped back. "You asshole!"

He grinned. "Much better than a handshake, wasn't it? No need to thank me."

And he was gone.

I stood there for a few moments.

As much as it sickened me mentally, physically, and metaphysically—

I was going to miss the bastard.

I was looking through all the containers in the fridge, deciding what to warm up for lunch, when the phone rang.

I grabbed it and continued with my food-finding mission. "Hello?"

"Maya." It was my mom, and she didn't sound happy. "Has Tahir left?"

"Yeah about twenty minutes ago."

"Your father and I are at Dimple's. We need to talk."

I promptly lost my appetite.

Chapter 33

AUNT DIMPLE and Uncle Pradeep lived in Anaheim Hills.

Once, when I was a kid, I made the mistake of referring to the area as just Anaheim in front of my aunt. A long lecture ensued on the difference between The Hills and the rest of the city.

I couldn't understand what the big deal was. So what if she lived in Anaheim Hills? It was still north Orange County, and everyone knew south county, where we lived, was better.

Even though it was Sunday, it still took me thirty-five minutes to get to her house. In Southern California, social conversation revolved around—not politics and the weather—but freeway changes, driving times, and traffic patterns. Whoever had to change the most freeways in order to get to a place won.

Homes in Anaheim Hills were mansionlike, and the neighborhoods had an attractive woodsy feel.

But I'd never move there.

I needed to be within walking distance of the beach.

I drove up a long windy driveway that diverged at the top. On the right was my aunt's house. I parked behind my mom's silver Mercedes, then rang the doorbell.

I knew what this was about.

Tahir had moved out, and it didn't take a nifty third eye to see that nothing had happened between us—our earlier lip lock notwithstanding.

Aunt Dimple opened the door and instead of her usual exuberant hug, she wore a very familiar pinched expression.

Apparently it was contagious.

"We've been expecting you," she said.

I stepped into the hall. The door shut behind me with a dull hollow thud.

I wondered if I'd ever see daylight again.

I was sitting in the middle of a cream-colored sofa.

Across from me on an identical piece of furniture, were my mom and aunt. Between us was a glass-and-teakwood coffee table Aunt Dimple had purchased on her last trip to India. The same trip where she acquired a husband for yours truly.

After shooting me a fatherly look of disapproval and murmuring something about potential, my dad left the room, a copy of *Investor's Business Daily* tucked under his arm and a cup of tea in his hand.

No one offered me any tea.

I needed to think of something, anything, to distract

my mom and aunt from their appointed topic. My gaze alighted on a new throw rug.

Aunt Dimple had a passion for redecorating. The house was done up on a monthly basis. Since her children were married with homes of their own, and Uncle Pradeep was fairly easygoing unless you brought up proctology, there was no one to complain about the constant upheaval.

Currently the decorating theme was Indian, hence the coffee table. Now that Indian culture was trendy again— even among actual Indians—consumers were rushing about in a state of monsoon madness, demanding anything and everything Indian. There was a bronze Ganesh on the mantel above the fireplace, heaps of embroidered cushions covered in mirror work, sandalwood boxes, incense holders, and carpets galore.

With the exception of the coffee table, I was betting everything was from Pier 1 Imports.

"Hey," I said with forced interest, "is the throw rug new?"

The pinched expression vanished from my aunt's face and was instantly replaced with her familiar cherubic smile. "I just bought it yesterday. The matching pillows are still upstairs. I'll get—" She stopped at my mom's look.

My cunning plan for distraction had failed.

"Now, Maya, tell us exactly what's going on between you and Tahir," my mom commanded.

I was so tempted to lie.

In fact, it would be easy to blame it all on Tahir. Pretend to be hurt over his indifference and all that gut-wrenching stuff. But there were two things wrong with that idea. One, it would get back to Tahir, and his gloating would transport me to the seventh realm of Hell, and two, I had to act like an adult occasionally. I would tell the truth.

But not about the goddess thing.

"We're not interested in each other," I began. What I wanted to do with his supple and taut body had no bearing on this conversation. "How could we be? You don't bring two strangers together and expect them to like each other instantly."

My aunt's face took on a baffled expression. "What strangers? Which strangers? I've met his parents. I've seen his astrological chart. You two are a perfect match!"

"But that's just it. How can we be a perfect match when we don't even know each other?"

"You didn't take the time to know him," my mom argued. "Leaving him alone in the restaurant. Running away from the party Gayatri gave especially for you—" A gasp from my aunt made her stop.

Aunt Dimple's hand was clamped to her mouth. Her eyes were filled with hurt. Slowly she lowered her hand. "I knew none of this! Maya, how could you? Do you know how hard I worked to make Tahir's mother agree to this match? Do you know what I did? I—I *lied*!"

"About what?" I asked.

"I told her you were twenty-five."

"But Tahir knows how old I am. I told him."

Hand pressed to her forehead, Aunt Dimple fell back against the cushions. "All hope is now lost."

My mom ignored her sister-in-law's theatrics. "Can you at least appreciate how worried your father and I are about you?" My dad strolled into the room, grabbed the plate of cookies, and left. "You won't get married. You spend all your time shopping, going to the salon, and doing God knows what."

I opened my mouth to tell her about my new and exciting career, and stopped. Her worry would surely be exacerbated after discovering the fate of the world was in my hands. Not to mention the fact there was a fanatic out there trying on a regular basis to obliterate me.

Besides, I didn't need her criticizing my malevolence-fighting techniques.

"Mom, please understand that I'm not against marriage. If a great guy comes along, I'm not going to turn him away, but neither am I going to rush into something I'm not ready for. I don't feel like there's this biological clock ticking away or anything."

"Let's call Gayatri," my aunt said from the depths of the cushions.

"I already know the ovaries deal," I said quickly. "But I'm not going to live my life by reproductive ability alone. And I'm not going to agree to a marriage for marriage's sake. What about shakti? What about female power?"

My mom and aunt stared back at me. They obviously weren't feeling the shakti.

"If you wait too long, all you'll have left to choose from are widowers and divorcées," Aunt Dimple pointed out helpfully.

Ganesh, get me out of here!

My mom sighed. "We're at a loss, Maya. Your father and I have decided to give you thirty days to prove you're serious about your life. Or"—she shook her head sadly—"you're out of the house."

Aunt Dimple finally sat up. "Don't worry, you can stay with me."

My mom glared at her. "No! This is her chance to prove I did not raise a lazy good-for-nothing."

Great. Just great. I should never have let her buy that dumb Dr. Phil book.

Aunt Dimple winked at me, using half her face. "I could use a receptionist at the office. The pay is excellent."

"Absolutely not," my mom said. "There will be no help from the family. Maya must try on her own."

There she sat. Knees together. Hands folded in her lap. Lips pressed into a straight line.

Instead of a coffee table, I felt like a chasm separated us. Somehow I needed to bridge that emotional divide.

Aunt Dimple caught my eye and smiled hopefully. "How about some tea?"

Too little caffeine.

Too late.

Chapter 34

MY PARENTS OPTED to have dinner at Aunt Dimple's.

I opted to drive away like a bat out of hell.

Then I opted for In & Out.

Sitting alone at the kitchen table, staring at a french fry, I pondered my possibilities.

I'd never planned for anything in my life, preferring to coast along and deal with things as they came. I'd never had any ambitions or dreams.

I wasn't like my brother Samir, who would cuddle up between my parents on the sofa to watch open-heart surgery on the Discovery Channel. There was never any question he would be a doctor.

Big surprise, we weren't the closest of siblings.

I felt lost and confused. I felt as though I'd made a mess of my life. I wished I'd studied harder so I could have gone to Harvard or bicycled through Cambridge.

You know, interesting shit like that.

Now I was supposed to look for a career, prove to my parents I could take care of myself, and all in thirty days?

Between sleeping and fighting evil, I had like two or three hours a day free.

I still couldn't believe my parents were kicking me out. There was nothing I could do for now but go along and hope something would happen in the next thirty days to make them change their minds—something other than my unnatural and painful death of course.

If not, I'd just move in with Ram and Sanjay. They were the ones who got me into this mess.

I wasn't even going to entertain the idea of asking Tahir if he needed a roomie—regardless of how rich with enticing possibilities that scenario might prove to be.

It was dark outside, and my fries were cold.

Was that a killer beginning to a depressing novel or what?

That night I woke up shivering.

Somehow I'd kicked off all the covers. Then I remembered the dream. I was in an advanced kickboxing class. Only instead of a punching bag, I was practicing on Nadia.

Reaching for the comforter, I heard the sound of the television. I peered at the digital alarm clock—3:00 A.M.

Slipping into my robe, I went downstairs. My mom was curled up on the couch watching CNN.

She looked tired. She looked older than her age. I felt my throat tightening.

She was awake because of me.

"Mom?" I said softly, walking toward her.

She didn't answer.

I moved closer and laid a hand on her shoulder. "I'm sorry, Mom . . . about Tahir. Please don't worry." I struggled to think of the right words to put her at ease. "I'm going to make some changes. Not just because of what we talked about earlier . . . I've been looking at my life lately and believe me, I've been seeing things in a whole new light. Just don't worry, okay?"

She didn't turn around. "Go to sleep, Maya. It's late."

I removed my hand and stepped back.

She didn't believe me.

I felt my heart drop.

The Asha Patels of the world could take control of their lives, but not the Maya Mehras. Women like me had only one hope, marriage. We weren't smart enough or strong enough to make it on our own.

I could see where she was coming from. My parents were getting older. She was afraid. Afraid of what would happen to me after they were gone. Who would take care of me? In her heart she truly felt I could not take care of myself.

I understood it. But her lack of faith hurt.

Hurt me in ways malevolence never could.

I didn't know what to say. I didn't know how to convince her.

Then, silent and weightless, Ram's words floated to the surface of my mind. *Kali is bound with the terrifying, and she is unafraid.*

Kali was part of me, too.

Sonia Singh

It was time to face my biggest fear.
It was time to grow up.
I would show my parents. I would show myself.
Can you imagine Maya Mehra doing that?
Damn straight!
Quietly, I left the room.

Chapter 35

NOW I'VE SEEN ENOUGH horror movies to know not to enter an abandoned warehouse alone and at night.

But I wasn't some screaming bimbo with clothes torn in all the right places. I was the goddess.

Still . . .

This smelled fishy. But that could be due to the close proximity of the Long Beach docks.

The rusted sign hanging above the entrance read: BROWNFIELD & COMPANY. I wondered what happened to old Brownfield. Located conveniently next to the port and freeway, and away from residential areas, abandoned warehouses like this one had once provided a service.

Personally, I thought the area had potential. Convert the derelict buildings into a series of trendy lofts. With the fabulous ocean view, they'd fetch quite a price. Of course there was the dead fish smell, but that could be handled by gearing the place toward stuffy-nosed allergy sufferers.

Oh well, it wasn't like some real estate development committee was hanging on my every word.

I turned my attention back to the door. The perps were inside, and I was spoiling for a fight.

Another Saturday night sans plans—of the social variety—had put me in a grumpy mood. The fact that I had sent my résumé out to companies all across the board with no response hadn't helped either. Apparently a BA in anthropology and no work experience didn't exactly open any doors.

I called the Goddess Within, waited for the lightning, then kicked the door down.

And Tahir thought I needed to go to the gym?

Two guys—one white, one black—whirled to face me, guns outstretched.

Maybe next time I should try stealth.

My divine instincts kicked in, and I dived to the floor just as they fired.

Guns. Why did it always have to be guns?

The NRA was seriously making my job harder than it had to be.

I was already irritated, and the fluorescent lighting was doing nothing for my complexion.

From my position on the floor, I thrust up with the sword and swung at the guns, knocking them out of their hands.

Then I had another idea.

In the two weeks since the Kathak concert, I'd become quite adept at handling the sword. The more I used it, the more it seemed like an extension of my arm.

I sliced out again, in a move straight out of *Zorro*.

Their pants dropped, tangled up with their feet, and they simultaneously tripped and fell.

Hmm, so they both preferred boxers.

I tied them up, back to back, with some rope I found in the warehouse. Seated on the floor, the black guy and the white guy stared up at me with extreme dislike.

Ebony and Ivory live together in perfect malevolency . . .

I used one of their cell phones to call the police.

While I waited for the sound of sirens, I examined the contents of the dozens of boxes stacked everywhere. I still had no idea why I'd followed these guys all the way from Newport to Long Beach.

The boxes were filled with guns.

Of course.

Speaking of firearms, I decided to dump theirs into the harbor. Not exactly an environmentally friendly plan but efficient. As I leaned over to scoop up his gun from the floor, the white guy snarled in my face. "Fucking camel jockey."

How original.

"Technically that slur would apply to Bedouins since only about half a percent of Indians actually travel by camel," I pointed out.

They both stared at me blankly.

Sirens wailed in the distance. Finally! I was so ready to be gone.

*   *   *

Back in the car, I realized my cell phone had been turned off all day. I switched it on.

Not one call.

Okay, I hadn't expected any calls from home. Ever since the ultimatum at Aunt Dimple's, my mom wasn't exactly speaking to me.

I scrolled down my list of numbers. Tahir's name popped up.

He'd called once, since moving out, wanting to know if there was a Neiman Marcus in Santa Monica. Before I could inform him the closest was in Beverly Hills, he received another call and put me on hold.

After three minutes I hung up.

But saved his number.

Instead of examining my motives behind that decision, I scrolled up to Ram. I'd left him numerous messages, but he hadn't called me back in days. Instead of feeling worried about the old man, I was irritated. The last time we'd spoken Ram had been in the middle of his current favorite TV show, *The Sopranos*. Apparently the fate of the world could wait, and he asked me to call back.

The pundit had a penchant for prime time.

Screw that! I needed to talk. I felt like I was operating in a vacuum. I had no feedback. No way of knowing whether I was doing a good job or not. Wondering if what I was doing had any relevance in the long term.

I dialed Ram.

After five rings Sanjay's voice came on the machine.

This time I was going to speak my mind. I didn't care who overheard. If Sanjay was entertaining Maury Povich at the moment, that was his goddamn problem.

"Hi, Ram, this is Maya. The goddess, remember? I want to know how stopping all these individual crimes is supposed to save the world from destruction? I don't see the pattern." I paused. "Oh yeah, and the Kali-hating fanatic seems to have gone underground. No attempts to murder me in a week. *Ciao.*" I hung up and sat back.

Apparently, even my archenemy had plans on a Saturday night.

Along with the rest of the world.

Lately I'd been engaging in a lot of serious soul-searching and basic internal delving. I'd been examining those issues in my life that were holding me back. Issues that kept me from having fulfilling relationships with men, women, my family, God, animals, and the Starbucks employees I saw every morning.

You know, meditating on my misconceptions.

Maybe I'd spend the rest of the night doing some more of that?

Nah.

I'd rather feel sorry for myself.

Here I was saving the world, and no one cared. There was only one thing to do at a time like this.

Drink.

After all, what went better with self-pity than alcohol?

Chapter 36

THE GODDESS was an alcoholic.

How else could you explain the fact that I'd knocked back three dirty vodka martinis and wasn't feeling a thing?

The bartender pointed at my glass. "Another?"

"Yessh pleashe."

Okay, maybe I was feeling something.

Either that or I was unintentionally doing a really bad impersonation of Sean Connery.

The White Lotus, my favorite LA nightspot, was packed. The tables were draped with trendy types and striving starlets. In the center of a fountain an enormous statue of Buddha gazed benevolently down at the scene.

The Goddess Gaze had worked wonders on the bouncer.

Normally I didn't have a problem getting in, but this was Saturday night, and I was dressed in jeans—the better to fight malevolence with. Cameron Diaz, whom I'd spotted earlier, might have been able to gain entrance dressed in flip-flops and a sack made out of hemp, but I wasn't some pampered celebrity.

As much as I wanted to be.

"Hard day?" the guy next to me said, taking a seat. He had wide blue eyes, red hair, and perfect eyebrows.

This was LA. Men waxed, plucked, and highlighted with the best of us.

Even though Orange County was a mere forty-five minutes away, I'd left the land of Christian Conservatives far behind, having crossed into the territory of Celebrity Culture.

Both regions had their plus points.

LA had hipness. Orange County had parking.

I checked out Perfect Brows, as the bartender set another frosty glass in front of me. "Today was a bitch. I had to work."

He was checking me out as well. "What do you do?"

"I'm Kali. Goddess of Death and Destruction. Giver of Life and Devourer of Children."

Oops.

Alcohol hadn't loosened my tongue; it had completely unhinged it.

"Kali, huh. The chick with all the arms, right?" He nodded, taking a sip of his drink. "My guru mentioned her. Have you heard of the Art of Living? My guru says . . ."

I tuned out.

Another Hare Krishna Hippie Freak, as Nadia would say.

I popped an olive into my mouth and blinked at my glass. It was empty. I picked up the glass and turned it upside down, staring in puzzlement as not a single drop fell out.

Perfect Brows was saying something. "So do you have a one-woman show?"

"Huh?" I was having trouble focusing. What the hell was he talking about? And then my alcohol-imbibing brain cells got it. He thought I was an actress. As in, I'm not a goddess but I play one on TV. "No, I'm the real deal. Really."

He stared at me.

"You think I'm crazy, don't you?" I said.

"Not at all. You know the guy on the corner of La Cienega and Sunset? The one who's always screaming he's Jesus? Everyone ignores him, but one day I started to think, what if the dude's telling the truth? I mean, if Jesus really did come back and stood on a street corner sermoning away, of course people would think he's Michael-Jackson-mental." He signaled the bartender. "One more round."

Between the two of us we were shelling out quite a bit for drinks. The White Lotus wasn't cheap.

Cheaper than therapy though.

Perfect Brows was staring at me with a definite glint in his eye. He had superb taste. I'd give him that. And since I wasn't Michael-Jackson-mental, he'd probably try to get in my pants.

"Wanna dance?" he said.

"Sure." I slid off the stool.

And promptly fell to the floor.

The next morning my head was hammering and my throat was drier than British humor.

Divine healing, my ass.

And then I forgot about all that.

I was in a strange bed, in a strange room.

Naked.

The body beside me shifted and pressed against my side.

Very definitely male.

I covered my face with my hands. Shit! I'd gone home with Perfect Brows.

And I couldn't remember any of it.

"Morning-after regrets? It's a bit too early for a cliché, don't you think?" a familiar voice drawled.

My hands flew off my face and I turned to stare at the very sleepy, very sexy man next to me.

Tahir.

Oh, Goddess!

It was worse than I thought.

Chapter 37

"I CAN FEEL your heartbeat," Tahir murmured.

"I didn't realize it was between my legs," I snapped, and leaped off the bed, wrapping the sheet around me so fast the room whirled.

"How did this happen?" I demanded.

Arms crossed behind his head, Tahir watched me with amusement. "Girl meets boy. Girl gets piss drunk. Girl calls boy to pick her up. Girl jumps boy and tears his clothes off."

I forced myself to remember. Dancing in a crowd. Losing sight of Perfect Brows. Calling Tahir because I was too drunk to drive.

Calling Tahir . . .

Cell phones were a nuisance and should definitely be banned. I would take up the cause immediately.

Girl suddenly recalls intimate details of the night before.

I sneaked a sideways glance at Tahir. He lounged on the bed like a well-sated Mughal emperor and stared back at me with frank approval.

I couldn't help the spark of pride that flared up inside me.

Maybe I'd been channeling Kali. Maybe I'd been feeling the shakti. Or maybe it was true that a woman's libido went into overdrive after the age of thirty. But I'd never been that uninhibited or abandoned before.

Whatever the case—

The goddess was pretty damn good in the sack!

Soothed by thoughts of my sexual prowess, I was able to take in the details of the room around me. White walls. Black furniture. Hardwood floor. Atop the dresser, a collection of photos in elegant silver frames caught my eye.

Affecting an air of French sophistication—so we had sex, big deal—I strolled over to the dresser.

In the first one, Tahir was wearing a cap and gown and standing between two older people. "Your parents?" I asked.

Tahir sat up, black silk sheets pooling around his legs, and peered over. "Yeah."

He didn't look like either one of them. His father was slight with delicate features and wispy gray hair. His mother was tall, heavyset, and dark. Her features were as formidable as her bosom. Instead of staring into the camera, she was gazing at her son with a look of rapt adoration. I suppressed a shudder and moved on.

The woman in the next picture was simply breathtaking. Her soft white hair was pulled back into a simple bun, exposing the long slender line of her throat. She wore a gold-embroidered sari and owned the chair as if it were a throne. Tahir looked exactly like her.

He stood up and my eyes immediately swung toward his nether regions, but he was wearing pajama bottoms the exact same color as the sheets. "My dadi." He picked up the frame, his expression softening as he gazed at his paternal grandmother. "I call her every Sunday."

"Who's this?" I pointed to a picture of a black Labrador drooling up into the camera, tail in midwag.

"Chum. Leaving him behind in Delhi was the hardest thing I had to do." Tahir's eyes were getting brighter by the moment. "My parents dote on him."

Any moment now I'd find myself with a weeping, half-naked man on my hands. I needed to snap him out of it. "So this is the softer side of Tahir?" I mocked. "Surprise. Surprise. And here I was thinking you had all the charm of Donald Rumsfeld coupled with the heart of Martha Stewart."

The corner of Tahir's mouth curled up in a smile. "You're in for another surprise. Take a look in the mirror."

What was it? A hickey the size of Long Island?

There was a funky, black, rectangular mirror—I was betting *Z Gallerie*—on the opposite wall. I walked toward it, looked, and nearly screamed.

A small ruby winked at me from the left side of my nose.

Holy shnoz! I'd gotten my nose pierced.

Tentatively, I reached out and touched it. "To reiterate, how did this happen?"

"A tattoo parlor on Main. We drove by, and you insisted on going in. They're known for their celebrity clientele. I think I saw Christina Aguilera being led into a back room."

Upscale tattoo parlor? Wasn't that a contradiction in terms? Trying to process the events of the night before left me feeling light-headed.

"I rather like it," Tahir added.

I snapped. Tahir's nonchalance had gone too far. "What kind of man are you? There I was, completely drunk, and you happily stand by while I get my nose pierced. Then you happily have sex with me afterward."

Tahir ran a hand through his hair. "We came back here, and I had a few drinks myself—I'm not making excuses—but," he paused, "there is such a thing as personal responsibility."

I was still formulating a witty reply when he reached over and brushed a lock of hair off my bare shoulder. "Listen. Last night was amazing, and I know it wasn't because of the alcohol. This thing between us"—his warm hands slid up my arms and rested on my shoulders—"is rare and real."

The room was suddenly hotter than August in India.

Tahir was waiting. The moment was pregnant with intimacy. I would have to weigh my next few words carefully.

"Did you use protection?" I asked.

Damn.

That wasn't what I'd meant to say.

He stepped back, hands dropping to his sides. "Yes, of course."

"Umm, great." I quickly began retrieving my clothes from the floor. Arms full, I raced for the door next to me and whipped it open, praying it was the bathroom and not the closet.

'Cause I didn't want to look stupid.

Make that stupider.

Confronted with marble, I let out a sigh of relief. Bathroom. Without looking at Tahir, I slammed the door shut and locked it.

Sinking to the edge of the tub, I buried my face in my hands and willed the image of Tahir, arms at his side, expression hurt, out of my head.

Well, what did he expect me to say?

I didn't know how I felt about him. I knew I wanted him. I missed him when he was gone. But that could all be lust. I mean, if Tahir had one eye and lurched around like the hunchback of Notre Dame, would I still feel the same way?

I really, really wanted him.

Yesterday I'd been complaining. I'd felt lonely. Was I saving the world or wasn't I saving the world, and did anyone care?

Outside Tahir was waiting to take me in his arms, and at the moment it was the only place I wanted to be.

I felt the Universe was giving me a sign.

I opened the door.

Tahir was in the middle of the room, clad in a pair of jeans, and pulling on a shirt.

I cleared my throat. "I'm up for exploring this connection between us, what about you?"

The next moment his mouth was against mine.

Oh yeah.

This time, I was going to remember each and every second of it.

Chapter 38

I WAS DEFINITELY feeling the shakti.

I was back in my car, singing along with Lauryn Hill at the top of my lungs. It was well into evening and dark outside. Tahir had wanted to take me to Dolce for dinner. I'd been sorely tempted—by Tahir and the meal—but I had a job to do, malevolence to battle.

Even though we were now lovers—a giggle escaped my lips—I hadn't told Tahir about the goddess thing. First of all, how do you bring something like that into casual conversation? I mean, that would require the mother of all smooth transitions. Secondly, if I did tell him, would he believe me? I was having trouble believing it, and I had lightning at my beck and call. Third, what if I did call up the winds, and I ended up scaring the shit out of him? He'd hightail it away so fast, Speedy Gonzales couldn't keep up with him.

I liked having Tahir in my life. I didn't exactly know what the status of our relationship was—somewhere between fuck buddies and dating—but I didn't want to risk it.

And that sort of brought me to why I hadn't told my parents the truth yet. In the beginning it was the normal dysfunctional-family, don't-ask-don't-tell thing, but now it had evolved into something else.

I was afraid to tell them.

I was afraid of seeing the fear and incomprehension on their faces. We had enough problems as it was. I didn't want them looking at me as some kind of monster.

It was well and good worshipping a deity from a distance. But even the most peaceful Buddhists residing in the state of Zendom would find it a bit unsettling if their son turned out to be the incarnation of Buddha. They might even hang themselves from the nearest Bodhi tree.

The truth could wait.

For the moment my holy secret was safe with me.

But there was one thing I couldn't wait for. With Tahir I'd found an even better workout than fighting evil. And I was hungry. I was more than hungry.

In the words of Mohandas K. Gandhi, after his famous fast ended, "Can someone get me some goddamn food?"

I was in the drive-thru of Carl's Jr. ordering a Western Bacon cheeseburger meal, when my cell phone rang.

Ram was finally calling me back.

"Where've you been?" I demanded. "Can I get criss-cut fries instead of regular?"

"Crisscross?" Ram asked.

"Hold on." I finished ordering, then moved ahead into

the long line of cars leading up to the window. I settled back and turned my attention to Ram. "Sorry about that. Now why haven't you called?"

"I was on holiday in Seattle."

"Seattle?"

"Sanjay had work there. It was a most joyous trip. We went to the Space Needle, but I lost my sandal at Pike Place Market."

"Why didn't you tell me you'd be out of town?"

Ram sounded genuinely puzzled. "I did not think you would be so distressed. I mailed you a postcard," he added.

I couldn't help smiling. "Thanks. Now we definitely need to meet. I have a couple of questions for you."

"That is acceptable. Sanjay is with Indira. We can meet here." His voice dropped to a whisper even though he'd just said he was alone. "I do not think Indira likes me. She looks at me like she is a sleeping cobra, and I am the annoying little boy who has been poking her with a stick trying to rouse her from her slumber."

I laughed. "I don't think she's too into me either. Listen, I'm in LA. I should be in Irvine in about forty minutes."

"Let it be so," Ram said, and hung up.

I paid and merged back into traffic. Burger in one hand, fries in the other, and steering with my elbows. Just as I took a bite my cell rang again.

Tahir's name flashed across the screen.

A thrill ran through me.

Taking one elbow off the wheel, I shoved the burger, complete with wrapper, into my mouth to hold, and grabbed the phone.

It slipped and fell between my feet.

I tried to grab it with my foot, but not even I was that coordinated.

Reluctantly, I made a right and pulled into a residential street. By the time I picked up the phone, he'd hung up.

I was about to call him back, when there was a loud crash and I was thrown forward onto the steering wheel.

My car had been hit from behind.

Fuming, I yanked open the door and jumped out. No one, but no one, dented my H2. If they didn't have insurance, I would descend on them with all the force of my sacred right to rage.

And then the malevolence hit.

Ugh.

This wasn't some innocent driver.

The malevolence was strong, distinct. I'd come to realize that malevolence was as unique to the individual as body odor.

Ugh.

As in body odor ugh. Not evil ugh.

Actually, the malevolence was more than distinct. It was familiar. I'd felt it before at Aunt Gayatri's party and periodically afterward.

The Kali-hater was back.

Before I could open the door and retrieve my sword, he was in front of me.

My hand froze on the door handle.

What shocked me wasn't the gun pointed at my mid-section. I was used to guns.

My stalker moved closer and the light from the street-lamp fell on his face, illuminating what I'd already seen.

I couldn't believe it.

The Kali-hater was none other than Ram's cousin.

Mild-mannered computer programmer—

Sanjay.

Chapter 39

"SO THIS WHOLE TIME I've been pursued by Dilbert with a tan? Well, now I know why all the attempts on my life failed."

Okay, maybe it wasn't such a good idea to insult the person who currently had a gun trained on yours truly, but Sanjay had started it. He'd made fun of my driving, and now he wanted me dead.

His hand tightened on the gun. "You are the embodiment of evil and must be destroyed."

I rolled my eyes. "Whatever. No wonder I had a relatively calm week. You were in Seattle."

Sanjay's eyes—already gleaming with fanaticism—took on an even more fervent flash. "After I dispose of you, I will remove the second most evil person on Earth—Bill Gates. And my software program to rival Windows will finally stand a chance."

The dude was seriously wacked.

Well not about Bill Gates—most Americans probably found him to be a wee bit evil—but definitely about me.

"Why are you after me? I don't get it." In movies the hero usually kept the villain talking as long as possible. Seemed like a plan to me, until I thought of something else. "You're Hindu, and Kali is a revered Hindu goddess."

There was a soft thump, and an orange cat with white paws curled up on the hood of my car and stared at us with interest.

Sanjay didn't seem to notice our four-legged observer, too preoccupied, as he was, with thoughts of eradicating my existence. "The gods created Kali to destroy the Demon King, but she became far worse than any monster she slaughtered. Kali feeds on death. She was reborn, not to save the world, but to destroy it."

For a Hindu, I could not believe how off the mark Sanjay was. Then again, that was sort of the definition of fanatic, wasn't it? I had heard of a cult in Calcutta that supposedly conducted human sacrifices in the name of Kali—a problem I'd definitely have to address—but that was like blaming Jesus Christ for the Spanish Inquisition.

I looked over at the cat. I wondered if my powers extended to communicating with animals? I stared, willing the creature to leap onto Sanjay's face and claw his eyes out. Instead it began licking its paw.

Fine. So I couldn't count on a feline sidekick.

"But why come after me now, Sanjay? You were trailing me for days before Ram arrived from India. Why not take me out then?"

Sanjay shrugged. "I had to make sure you were the one. And frankly, I had my doubts until the end."

"But why—"

"Enough!" he shouted. "Tonight it ends. Your death will restore the balance of the world."

Ram and Sanjay kept throwing that phrase "balance of the world" around, and I still didn't get what it meant.

"Sanjay, listen," I began.

"I am only the first step," he said. "You will be punished well into your next life. The karmic wheel of justice shall see to that."

"Punished how? Am I gonna come back looking like you?"

"Here kitty, kitty."

Sanjay and I both turned to see an old woman in fuzzy slippers and matching robe, step out onto the porch. "Here kitty, Jeff kitty." She spotted us and stared suspiciously.

Two brown people in an upper-middle-class neighborhood will do that.

"Who's there?" she called out.

I used that moment to call the Goddess Within.

Lightning flared against the sky.

Gun raised, Sanjay whipped around to face me.

With its fur standing on end, the cat rose on all fours, hissed, and sped away.

Sanjay started, distracted by the cat. I lunged and kicked him in the face. Not too difficult since he was only a couple inches taller than I.

He screamed and fell back, dropping the gun and clutching his nose.

The leg weights were paying off.

I picked up the gun. I'd dispose of it in the nearest body of water. I was chucking guns into the ocean on a regular basis. If malevolence didn't get me, the EPA surely would.

The old lady was peering from her porch. "What's going on? I'm calling the police." She hurried back into the house.

Sanjay jumped up, hand still pressed to his bloodied nose—I was betting I'd broken it—and took off running, darting between two houses and disappearing into the shadows.

I debated my options.

I could go after Sanjay or get the hell out before the police arrived.

I elected to do the latter.

As I opened the door of my car, I heard a soft meow. Jeff the cat was sitting on the grass watching me. His golden eyes caught the light.

He looked distinctly unimpressed.

Sanjay's apartment smelled like IKEA.

Ram sat silently as I poured out my tale. When I reached the end, he stood and excused himself.

He went into the bedroom and returned carrying a small beaten satchel. "Naturally I choose no longer to cohabit with malevolence."

Naturally.

I was about to get us both out of there when a thought struck me with all the force of Fat Albert. "Ram, why didn't my Malevolent Meter ever go off around Sanjay? Like that first night at the Holiday Inn and all the other times when he wasn't trying to exterminate me?"

"The first night we met you were not open to the Goddess Within," Ram replied. "And later Sanjay knew of your abilities. He guarded his thoughts and emotions carefully around you. As a very young man he spent months with the ascetics in the hills. He is able to control his body and mind to a stunning degree. What more Sanjay learned, he has always kept to himself."

I resisted the urge to stamp my foot. "What is up with all these loopholes? Sanjay can walk around in some sort of zombie state, and I won't know a thing until he's about to strike?"

"There is no reason for you not to be completely aware of Sanjay at all times."

"Oh." I felt the relief slide over me. "So how exactly . . ." My voice trailed off as I recognized what Ram truly meant. "Don't give me that again! I don't know what would have happened tonight if that batty old lady hadn't come out looking for her cat. Next time Sanjay will probably just shoot me in the back of the head. I don't have time to seek enlightenment!"

Ram's face took on a look of supreme patience. "Now more than ever you must believe these—loopholes as you say—are only in your mind. You must break through the mental barriers you have constructed."

I was trying, honestly I was, but apparently I needed to hurry.

"Therapy under pressure. I get it." Opening the front door, I gestured for Ram to precede me. "Let's get the hell out of here. I'll check you into a hotel."

Ram swept by me with a swish of his orange robe. "A hotel is unnecessary. I will stay with you."

I blanched. "I don't know, Ram. My parents . . ."

"It will be fine," he said.

End of discussion.

I shut the door behind me with a bang.

Ram, my parents, and me, all under one roof.

Sure.

It'd be fun.

A curry-scented breeze.

Not.

Chapter 40

MOM WAS IN FRONT of the TV watching the latest Bolly-wood blockbuster.

Nowadays it was possible to see the DVD version of the newest Hindi flick just days after it was released in India.

Wasn't piracy grand?

On-screen the hero and heroine were passionately embracing on top of the Swiss Alps, passionately gazing into each other's eyes in the middle of rolling green meadows, then passionately necking in a bed of brilliantly colored tulips. The heroine wore a seductively skimpy sari and the hero—a transparent black shirt that showed off his studly brown nipples.

"I've seen this movie," I said by way of greeting.

My mom answered without looking up. "No, you haven't."

At least she was talking to me. Her maternal deep freeze was apparently set on thaw.

"Yeah, I have. They're in Switzerland, right? The girl's

father is a billionaire industrialist who keeps trying to kill the hero because he's poor."

"It's a different movie," she insisted. "In this one the heroine lives with her uncle—a billionaire industrialist— who keeps trying to kill the hero because he's from the wrong caste."

Ram nudged me. "The actress is very beautiful, no?"

My mom finally looked up, and her eyes widened.

Clearly the time was ripe for performing introductions.

"Mom—Ram. Ram—Mom." It almost sounded like a chant.

Ram folded his hands and inclined his head. "Namaste."

My mom rose from the couch. "Namaste."

I'd warned Ram in the car not to bring up the goddess thing and to let me do the talking. I cleared my throat. "Ram needs a place to stay. He was part of a temple exchange program, and his accommodations fell through."

My mom opened her mouth to respond when she caught sight of my nose ring. "You pierced your nose?"

I tried for chirpy. "Like it? Now I look just like you."

Switching to doctor mode, she marched over. "Where did you get it done? Is it infected?" She peered into my nostril. "I need a flashlight."

"Mom, it's fine."

Gently she touched the jewel. "This ruby is real."

"Apparently it was an upscale place."

Her eyebrows rose in suspicion as she switched back to

maternal mode. "Apparently? Where were you last night? The message you left on the machine was garbled."

I'd called? Even in my drunken haze, some ounce of self-preservation had obviously set in.

"Well?" She was still waiting for an answer. "Where were you last night?"

"I think Maya looks nice," Ram said.

I mentally blessed him, as my mom, recalling the presence of a guest, stepped back and smiled. "I'm sorry, punditji. We would be honored to have you as our guest."

Ram bowed his head in thanks.

Her gaze slid back to me, traces of suspicion still lingering. "How exactly did you and Ram meet?"

"Through the friend of a friend's cousin who's also a friend of mine. I figured it'd be a good way to get in touch with my Indian heritage. Ram's going to teach me meditation."

"Punditji," she corrected.

"What?"

"He is a holy man. Refer to him as punditji."

Ram agreed. "Yes, that is more appropriate."

I rolled my eyes. "Whatever."

My dad entered the room dressed in nothing but his boxers. Yawning and scratching his potbelly, he balked at the sight of us.

"Punditji will be staying here," my mom informed.

My dad performed the speediest Namaste in history and mumbled, "Very nice . . . most holiest of men . . . please enjoy . . . stay." The next moment he was gone.

"Where is the loo?" Ram asked.

After showing him the door, I found myself face-to-face with my mom again.

"Maya, there's something I need to discuss with you."

Automatically my mind raced through possible escape routes. Then I reminded myself of my vow to grow up and be an adult. So I stopped and waited for her to speak.

"Maya, I've been thinking about what I said to you at Dimple's, and it was a little strict. It's just . . . I worry about you . . ." Her voice trailed off.

I reached out to touch her—my mom and I didn't do hugs—when I thought what the hell and wrapped my arms around her.

She instantly stiffened, arms straight at her sides. Then slowly, I felt her relax. She didn't hug me back, but patted my shoulder and gently pulled away.

Okay, so it wasn't exactly a Hallmark moment, but it was a start.

"You weren't strict, Mom," I said. "You were right. I needed a push. I've sent out a bunch of applications for general office work and stuff."

"Office work?" She shot me an amused look. "Do you know how to type?"

I rolled my eyes. "Of course. With two fingers."

She smiled. "Your father and I are not going to kick you out. Why don't you look for something you really like to do?"

Hmm. What did I like to do? Shopping. Watching

movies. Watching television. I discarded eating, drinking, and sex, because they were pretty universal. Then again, so were movies and TV. Shopping? What about fighting malevolence? Sure, there was some job satisfaction, but . . . "It might take a while, Mom. I still haven't discovered the color of my parachute."

She sighed, but it was a good sigh. I could practically see the tension spill out of her. "As long as you're moving toward something—taking steps—that's all I want. If you decide to take some classes, we'll pay for them," she paused, "but it's a loan."

I laughed. "You're on."

"Well then, I'll get dinner ready for punditji."

"He's a vegetarian," I reminded.

She rolled her eyes. "Obviously."

Hey!

That was so my look.

Before going to bed, I crept downstairs to double-check that the alarm was activated.

My Malevolent Meter might not be able to detect Sanjay's presence, but Brinks definitely would.

Everything was in order.

I was tempted to turn on the upstairs motion detectors, but the guest bathroom was across the hall from the bedroom and I didn't know what sort of relationship Ram had with his bladder.

Satisfied that the house was safe and snug for the night, I let myself relax.

Tomorrow Ram and I were going to have a long talk about my powers.

My mystical Indian half was tempered by my practical, American, can-do half. Sure, enlightenment was one way to break down my mental walls.

A sledgehammer was another.

Chapter 41

MY WORLD had been turned upside down.

Literally.

I was propped up against the wall attempting Baddha-hasta Sirsasanai—the mother of all yogic headstands.

Not a good idea on a full stomach.

However, it was Ram's favorite posture, essential for uncovering the physical, emotional, and mental tensions held in the mind and body, thereby allowing insight to emerge.

Along with my lunch—if I kept it up.

"How much longer do we have to do this?" I complained. "My neck is killing me."

Ram, on the other hand, looked practically asleep. "A few more minutes," he murmured.

Coming downstairs that morning, I'd found my mom and Ram bonding over cups of tea. Apparently they shared a passion for Bollywood and were indulging in current celebrity gossip. Glossy film magazines, carried by the local Indian store, were spread out on the table before them. I caught a couple of the titles: *Filmfare, Stardust, CineBlitz.*

As I poured Zimbabwean coffee beans into the grinder—I don't do tea in the morning—their conversation turned to the Bollywood remake of *The Wedding Planner.*

"It was much better than the remake of *My Best Friend's Wedding,*" my mom said.

I shut the lid of the grinder. "I don't know about you guys, but I'm waiting for the Bollywood remake of *Schindler's List.*"

Blank looks from both.

Mom left for work soon afterward, and somewhere between breakfast and lunch, Ram convinced me to try meditation.

"Forget this!" I'd had it with headstands.

I just had to figure out how to return my body to its normal upright position.

Finally, I just let my legs sort of slide down the wall until I was horizontal, then I rolled over and sat up. While I ran my fingers through my hair, trying to fluff it up again, Ram executed a neat flip, with his legs curving over his head, his torso soon following, so that he was on his head one moment and in the crouching position the next.

The pundit was flexible. I'd give him that.

"Can we just do some normal meditating now?" I asked.

"As you wish," Ram replied. "We will continue outside."

We sat on the deck facing each other Indian-style. Although as Indians, any way we sat would technically be Indian-style.

For a winter afternoon, the day was clear and nice. A long-sleeved tee and jeans day.

Seven jeans of course.

"Should I call the Goddess Within?"

Ram adjusted the folds of his robe. "That is not necessary, we will focus on addressing your problem."

"Right—Sanjay."

"No. Sanjay is merely incidental. There will always be those who seek to end your life. Sanjay is most likely the first of many." He waved his hand like it was no big deal. "The problem is, you still have not found the courage to trust your talents."

"Well duh!" I tossed my hair and leaned back on my hands. "I'm sort of fighting evil here, not trying out for *American Idol*."

"Evil is not the source of your fear. This is." He tapped his head. "You are still calling the Goddess Within, though it should be a natural state you are in at all times. When you learn to combine your conscious and unconscious selves, you will be pure divinity."

"So what am I now, pure freak?"

He was about to answer when I held up my hand silencing him. "Okay, forget it. Moving on—I want to know exactly how I'm supposed to save the world from destruction. A date and time would be nice."

Ram smiled. "Only you know the answer to that question."

I wanted to punch him.

Unaware of my desire to do him bodily harm, he continued. "The goddess was born to save the world. I do not know how, when, or where. That is for you to discover."

I couldn't believe it. I was totally on my own.

Realizing he was slowly becoming adrift in my emotional undercurrents, Ram slid back a few inches. "What I *do know* is how I can help you become a fully actualized goddess. Through meditation."

Personally I preferred medication . . .

"Fine, let's get meditating."

"Close your eyes," Ram instructed.

I closed my eyes.

If you can't beat om.

Join om.

Chapter 42

SOME WOMEN will only sleep with a guy after the third date.

I slept with a guy before our first date.

Don't knock it till you try it.

Tahir was taking me to Tangiers, a hip restaurant in the trendy Los Feliz neighborhood of LA. It was our first official date.

I couldn't tell what I was more excited about. Seeing Tahir again, going to Tangiers, or actually having plans on a Saturday night. I suppose it was all of the above.

The old Maya was back.

I'd gotten my manicure and pedicure done, then headed to Ziba, a salon across the street from South Coast Plaza. I leaned back into the reclining chair as a woman approached me with a spool of cotton thread. Taking a deep breath, I closed my eyes.

Ziba specialized in threading, a beauty treatment/torture device where facial hair is removed with thread instead of wax. The beautician held one end of the thread in her teeth and the other end in her hand. With the available hand, she fashioned the middle of the thread into a loop. The loop trapped unwanted hair, which was then pulled from the skin.

One silent shriek at a time.

Threading had recently become popular in Southern California, even though it had been around for eons in India and the Middle East.

I was glad Indian culture had become trendy again. My mom didn't have to deal with people wondering if her red bindhi was really blood. And I didn't have people asking me questions like—Do you eat monkey brains? If I ever ran into Steven Spielberg, I'd let him know in alto terms how *The Temple of Doom* had led to plenty of negative stereotypes about Indians, not to mention Kali.

Who was I kidding? If I ever did meet him I'd probably blab how *E.T.* still made me sob.

Unfortunately, there was a downside to all this "trendiness" as well. Threading, which used to cost me five bucks, now cost fifteen. And if I ever wanted to get henna tattooing done—which I didn't because when it faded it resembled ringworm—I'd have to pay a whopping hundred dollars.

Thanks to celebs like Madonna, Gwen Stefani, and Naomi Campbell.

Still, with each yell-inducing yank of my brow hair, a thrill of happiness went through me. I felt like a normal chick again. Getting ready to go out with a total hottie.

I deserved a night out. Not just because I'd been saving the world (cross my fingers), but because of living with the cumulative annoyance of Mom and Ram.

Even though my mom and I had experienced a sort of breakthrough—I hugged her and she allowed it—that didn't mean we had stopped getting on each other's nerves. And now there was Ram.

The two were as thick as turbaned thieves.

Mom and Ram went to the Cerritos temple together on Tuesday night. Went to Little India for lunch on Wednesday to eat South Indian food. On Thursday they went to Disneyland. Ram now had Mickey Mouse ears to complement his robes. On Friday the Dish Network dude came and installed two Indian channels—Zee and Sony. From then on Mom and Ram were glued to the TV watching all the Indian soaps. Since it involved a couch, my dad joined them.

It wasn't like I was afraid they were having an affair. The problem was they were gossiping about me. Every time I entered a room, they'd stop talking and look at each other knowingly.

I dealt with this in the usual way, by getting out of the house. I had my regular meditation sessions with Ram, and the rest of my time was spent cruising around for criminals.

Oh yeah, and talking to Tahir on the phone.

It was weird not arguing or exchanging insults with him. It was even weirder thinking of us as a couple.

Wait. Were we a couple?

I didn't want to go that far. I hadn't even told my mom I was going out with Tahir because I didn't want to get her hopes up. We were having fun, and that was good enough for me. I didn't want to examine my feelings too strongly.

I wondered if Nadia was still chasing Tahir.

I wondered if Tahir was seeing other women.

I wondered if he was sleeping with other women.

I wondered if it was normal for a straight man to like shopping as much as I.

Okay, sometimes feelings didn't care whether you were ready to examine them or not.

The beautician pressed my shoulder. "Please, take a look."

I opened my eyes and gazed into the hand mirror she held in front of me, trying to ignore the ruby winking above my nostril. "You missed a hair, here." I pointed to my left brow.

Well, I needed the perfect brows to go with my perfect dress.

Settling back, I visualized my outfit for tonight—Dolce & Gabbana floral slip dress, matching Pashmina shawl, and my brand-new Manolo Blahnik ankle-wrap sandals. The clerk had smiled knowingly as she wrapped up my shoes. "Did you see these on *Sex and the City*?"

"I only watch the *McLaughlin Newshour*," I answered, and grabbed the bag. How dare she try to categorize me as some Carrie Bradshaw copycat! I'd been a fashionista from birth. My mom told me that as a toddler I'd once thrown a tantrum because the socks she put on me didn't match. One was eggshell, and the other was ecru. She didn't see the difference until I pointed it all out in belligerent baby speak.

Eyebrows finally arched to perfection, I went home to get ready.

Tahir and I met at his apartment—followed by some heavy breathing and my reapplication of lipstick—and from there he drove to the restaurant.

At the first red light, he let go of the gearshift and reached for my hand.

He held it until the light turned green.

We left the car with the valet and were heading up to the entrance when Tahir noticed a white Labrador waiting for its owner outside a shop. He walked over, crouched, and began rubbing the dog's ears, cooing into its face.

Hand holding? Dog petting?

Had Tahir undergone an exorcism recently or what?

A moment later he was back beside me. "You look amazing. Did I tell you that?" Wordlessly I shook my head no. He pulled me to his side. "Well, you do."

A sick feeling swelled inside me as we entered the restaurant. I hadn't felt this bad since my weeklong fling with amoebic dysentery on my last trip to India.

In the name of all that was holy and chargeable—

I knew what had happened.

I had fallen in love with Tahir.

Chapter 43

SOME PEOPLE found their peace in ashrams.

I preferred the toilet.

As soon as tactfully possible I excused myself from dinner to escape into the bathroom. Settling down into my porcelain sanctuary, I realized I was withdrawing to the WC on a regular basis.

Things had been going so well.

Why'd I have to ruin it by falling in love with him?

I tore off a sheet of toilet paper and began shredding it. What was wrong with me? The guy pets a dog, and suddenly I was Juliet Capulet. I tried vainly to convince myself that what I was feeling was just lust in warp drive, but even if Tahir were to gain fifty pounds (gulp) or mangle his face in a freak accident (gulp, gulp), I'd still feel the same way about him.

Call it love. Call it hysterical blindness. Whatever.

I didn't know what was more galling—falling in love with the man my family picked out for me—or falling in love with a man who'd explicitly stated he wanted a woman who respected her family and adhered to Indian values.

Regardless of what Tahir said, I believed I was just someone for him to fool around with until he found the perfect wife and mother for his future children.

Someone grabbed the stall handle and tugged.

"Occupied," I shouted.

I had enough pressure trying to figure out how to save the world, trying to keep my nails shiny and buffed, trying to meditate, trying to overcome childhood issues, trying to find a career path, and trying to stay alive while some computer programmer tried to kill me. . . .

And now this.

If only I knew how to micromanage my feelings.

Until then, I'd have to go back to my lamb shank and potatoes and face Tahir.

I stood and flushed the toilet for good measure. Exiting the stall I was confronted by a long line of ladies wearing the latest in dirty looks. I washed my hands, tossed my hair, and left the bathroom with my head held high.

Bathed in the soft glow of the candles, surrounded by golden walls and colorful carpets, we enjoyed our after-dinner grappa.

I was mulling over a restaurant idea of my own. Just in case the video game or the exercise video didn't take off. The cuisine would be California-Indian fusion. I even had a name. The Goddess Gourmet.

"Maya, are you listening?"

"Huh?" I looked over to see Tahir watching me expectantly. I straightened my shoulders and sat up. "Sorry, what were you saying?"

Tahir smiled. "I want to take back something I said to you before, because it wasn't the truth."

I went still. Could I have been wrong? Was Tahir going to admit he felt the same way about me, too? My cynicism melted under the warmth of requited love. Life suddenly pulsed with possibilities. Maybe I'd even vote in the next election.

"Maya." Tahir hesitated.

"Yes," I prompted.

He looked deep into my eyes. "Maya, I just want to say . . . I don't think you're crazy."

"What the—"

He interrupted. "I just wanted to share how I really felt."

I signaled the waiter. "Another shot of grappa, please."

He traced his finger down my palm. "I also think you're beautiful and original."

"Oh."

"One more thing . . ." His voice trailed off as the waiter set the shot glass down in front of me.

Compliment or insult? What would it be? I was going to have a massive coronary in the time it took for him to decide.

"Maya—"

Ugh.

Malevolence settled on me like one of Tangiers' thick Persian rugs.

Tahir squeezed my hand. "When I met you I—"

No. Not now. I wanted to squeeze his hand back. I wanted to hear what he had to say.

Ugh.

But I couldn't wait. Malevolence had beaten him to the punch.

"I have to . . . I'll be back." I slid out of the booth and began moving through the crowd. As the night had progressed, so had the crush of people.

I was at the door when Tahir whirled me around to face him. "What's wrong?" he demanded.

Whether he meant in the metaphysical or emotional sense, the explanation would take too long. "There's no time. I have to go."

"You can't do this again, Maya." His voice held an edge of finality.

I pulled away. "I'm sorry."

His expression was closed, his voice flat. "So am I."

I pushed my way out of the restaurant, refusing to look back.

What was I supposed to say?

Tahir had been right the day he'd moved out of our house.

It never would have worked out between us.

Chapter 44

MY LIFE HAD BECOME about running.

Running into bathrooms, running out the door, running in designer heels.

My Manolos!

I pulled them off, reducing my height by a good three inches, and scanned the street for malevolence.

Evil had taken a right.

Pashmina shawl flying behind me like a cape, I ran down the sidewalk in my bare feet, praying I wouldn't step in spit or shit.

This was seriously bad planning on my part. No sword. No Hummer. Nobody walked in LA. From now on I was taking my car everywhere—not that there'd be any more dates with Tahir.

Tahir. Best not to think about him.

My Malevolent Meter led me into a narrow alley, where a man had a woman up against the wall.

It didn't take a goddess to guess his intentions.

I was sick of evil in all its forms. Especially the nasty form that now stood in front of me.

I called the you-know-what within.

Lightning illuminated the gray eyes of the attacker, along with the shiny knife blade in his hand. The woman was slumped against the wall and made no move to get away.

There wasn't time to look for a clean place to set down my shawl and shoes, so I dropped them on the ground and grabbed the lid of a trash can.

"Who—" he uttered.

I flung the trash can lid as hard as I could, and divine accuracy took care of the rest.

The metal Frisbee caught him full in the face, and he hit the ground with a thud, a moment before the clattering disk.

He didn't move.

Maybe I'd been feeling a bit too much of the shakti?

I knelt at his side and felt for a pulse. It took me a few tries actually to find the correct spot—you'd think with a family full of doctors I'd detect it right away—but it was there, beating strong.

A groan made me turn my head and move toward the woman. She had long, streaked blond hair and a California tan. "Where's my date?" she murmured.

"Date?"

She took a step, fell toward me. I grabbed her. "The guy I picked up at the bar?" She was completely wasted, which made it all the more fun for me. "He said he wanted to show me something."

"Don't you watch the Lifetime Channel?" I asked. "They had a TV movie about this kind of thing just last week." I slipped one arm around her waist and used my other hand to pick up my stuff from the ground. After numerous falls and several stumbling steps, we managed to make it out of the alleyway.

"Where do you live?" I asked her.

She swayed. "I don't know. LA."

I rolled my eyes. "Where's your purse?" I could at least get her address from her driver's license.

"I had it in the bathroom when I was snorting." She stopped walking. "Don't feel good." Her eyes closed and she crumpled to the ground.

A woman with black hair and way too much makeup was unlocking the door to a Saturn at the curb.

Time to use the Goddess Gaze. "Hey!" She looked up. "I need to get to the hospital. Now."

She nodded. "Hospital . . . okay."

Together we heaved Blondie into the back of the car. I'd just saved her life. If she even thought of overdosing on me—

I'd kill her.

I left the waiting room as soon as the nurse assured me Blondie would be fine.

I decided to grab a cup of coffee. The hospital—Linda

Vista—was freezing. Wrapping my shawl around me, I followed the signs leading to the cafeteria.

I'd let the woman with the Saturn go, so I'd have to use the G.G. again later to get a ride to my car.

I was rounding the corner, the cafeteria in plain sight ahead when the doors to the elevator opened and a group of chattering nurses exited.

"What's up with Dr. Vargas?" one of them said, with a cross expression. "Ordering us around like we're servants?"

"Doctors," another said. "They strut around the hospital like they own it. 'M.D.' apparently stands for massive dick!"

"Not literally of course," another laughed.

"Don't we wish."

I couldn't see her face but a nurse in pink scrubs spoke up. "Come on, girls. Until we get more male nurses—nothing's going to change."

I froze in the corner. I knew that voice.

As they passed by me in the hall, I had a clear view of the group. My eyes widened. It was all I could do not to reveal my presence.

Suddenly, I didn't need the coffee after all. I'd completely perked up.

Thanks to the woman in pink.

As it turned out, my cousin Nadia wasn't a nephrologist after all.

She was a nurse.

Chapter 45

DO UNTO OTHERS, as you would have them do unto you.

Unless her name was Nadia and she was a total bitch.

In that case, you rub your hands in glee and ponder how to use her secret against her.

Hell, maybe I'd just call a press conference?

I'd found a ride. Dr. Saggar was cute, and he drove a BMW. He dropped me off in front of Tahir's complex and sped away with the blank, slightly cross-eyed look that seemed to be a symptom of the Goddess Gaze.

I was about to unlock my car door and get in when I stopped and stared up at Tahir's apartment building.

The old Maya would have gotten in her car and left.

The new Maya had a choice.

Maybe Tahir and I were really over, but maybe we weren't?

I bit my lip. I wanted people in my life. I wanted friends. I wanted Tahir. I had to try.

I had to take a chance.

Entering the lobby was one of the scariest things I'd ever done. Not vomit-inducing scary, but daunting nonetheless.

Kali binds herself to the terrifying, and she is unafraid.

I took a deep breath and pressed the buzzer.

His voice came through, curt and displeased. "Yes."

"Tahir . . . it's Maya."

Silence.

"There's something I have to tell you." I stopped. No more words. "Actually," I amended, "there's something I want to show you. Please, can you come outside?"

Instead of waiting for him to answer, I released the button. If Tahir didn't come down I'd keep ringing the buzzer until he called the police.

After a few minutes he was there, dressed in a T-shirt and sweats. "Well? What's the excuse now?"

"I want to show you who I really am."

He folded his arms. "Let me guess. You're actually a man."

"What?" I was horrified. "You've seen me naked!"

He shrugged. "Medical technology has improved by leaps and bounds."

"This isn't a transgender thing, Tahir. Just watch, please?"

I walked to the middle of the street—prayed no oncoming traffic would spoil the moment—and called the Goddess Within.

Streaks of lightning flashed in the sky as the familiar coil of warmth unfolded in my body. The wind came out of nowhere and churned around us. Ram had said the word for goddess in Hindi was 'devi': the Shining One. So I tried something new and visualized a white aura of light surrounding my body. It worked!

Apparently, the meditation really was freeing my mind.

Finally, I chanced a look at Tahir. He was watching me, his expression unreadable.

At least he hadn't peed himself.

Radiant light shone off my hands as I raised them. "I am the incarnation of Kali—the Dark Mother. My dharma is to save the world. So . . . ah . . . what do you think about that?"

"I don't think I've ever seen anything so bloody sexy in my life," he said.

I threw myself into his arms so hard I practically knocked him over.

After a few moments, Tahir said in a choked voice, "Maya, I can't breathe."

I loosened my grip from around his neck, thought what the hell, and blurted it out. "I love you."

He smiled smugly. "I thought so."

"Asshole."

He laughed. "I love you, too."

He leaned down to kiss me but I pulled back. "Wait. You don't seem very shocked about any of this Kali stuff."

"Growing up in India, I saw quite a bit of odd supernatural shit. Swamis levitating off the ground and so forth."

"Levitate? You're joking, right?" I wonder if Ram knew how to do any of that.

"Sweetheart, you just called up the forces of nature."

"You have a point."

He leaned down to kiss me again when I thought of something else. "What about looking for a good Indian wife and mother?"

"You're a good human being, and that's what matters most. That's what I wanted to tell you at the restaurant earlier." Before I could open my mouth again, he pulled me to him and brushed my lips with his. "Let's go inside."

Our arms around each other we walked up the drive. He swiped his key card and opened the lobby door. "Is that wind going to die down soon?"

Oops.

I turned back. "Stop!"

Thankfully it did. I would've been so totally embarrassed if it hadn't.

"Brilliant," Tahir said with admiration.

I grinned. "Tell me about it."

Chapter 46

THE LAST THING you'd want to think about when you're naked is your mom.

I sat up, pushed the hair out of my face, and squinted at the morning light filtering through the window. "Shit! I never called home."

"Hmm?" Tahir murmured next to me.

I leaned over him, grabbed the cordless off the bedside table, and dialed. The line was busy. We had call waiting, so after a moment I hit redial. Still busy. I hung up and called my mom's cell phone. Busy as well.

Huh.

I tried my dad's cell. Busy, busy, busy. Thinking they might be at work even though it was Sunday, I called their offices. No answer.

There was another way—thanks to the meditative exercises—and the rates were better than AT&T.

I closed my eyes and called the Goddess Within. I visualized my parents' faces. They were fine. I couldn't see into the house or zero in on what they were doing—this wasn't divine spy cam. I just got the sense that every-thing was okay.

Which didn't explain why all the phones in the house were being used.

Tahir yawned. "No luck?"

I looked at him over my bare shoulder. "You realize you are single-handedly destroying my reputation within the Indian community."

Tahir smiled lazily. "And enjoying every moment of it." I laughed, then his expression grew serious. "Speaking of phones, have you called the police about this Sanjay fellow? Maybe they can track him down?"

We'd stayed up late last night talking—and, uh, doing other things—and I'd filled him in on the life and times of Maya Mehra.

"If I tell the police about Sanjay, I'll have to answer a lot of uncomfortable questions. Next thing I know I'll be featured in a FOX Special like *Goddess Autopsy*. No way am I going to the police."

"What about that woman he was with at the Kathak concert?"

"Indira? I don't know her last name or where she works. Ram doesn't either."

Tahir raised himself on one elbow. "You know, for a goddess incarnate, you're severely limited in what you can do. Have you spoken to Ram about this?"

My eyes narrowed. "Don't even go there."

He began rubbing my arm in a soothing manner. "Subject is officially dropped. You know in India, it's quite the scandal for a single woman to spend the night at a man's house. It's practically unheard of."

"First Sanjay, now scandal, are you trying to get me in the mood?"

Tahir's response was decidedly cocky. "Don't worry about your parents. When they find out you and I are an item, they'll be thrilled."

I raised an eyebrow. "Consider yourself quite the catch, do you?"

Tahir matched me eyebrow for eyebrow. "Darling, I could be an ax murderer and still have my pick of proposals."

The goddess inside me stirred. Tahir needed to be taken down a notch.

I lunged.

When I let him up for air a while later, his bottom lip was bleeding.

"I worship you," he gasped.

I tossed my hair and smiled.

I wasn't going to allow any conversation after that.

After eating breakfast, I took a shower and came out of the bathroom in Tahir's robe to discover my clothes were nowhere in evidence.

I was peering under a chair for my apparel when Tahir walked into the room carrying a white plastic bag. "Have you seen my dress?" I lifted the comforter from the bed.

"It's folded and lying on the kitchen table," Tahir said.

"Do you usually lay out your clothes on the kitchen table?"

"Will you do something for me?"

"Like what?"

He rubbed his chin. "I have this thing. Well I guess you'd call it sort of a sexual fantasy. But I was wondering if you'd be willing to fulfill it?"

"Are you going to ask me to pee on your face?"

He looked taken aback. "No! That's disgusting."

"What is it? A little S&M?"

"Well you've just clued me in to your realm of fantasy." He removed the contents from the bag and held it up. A long shimmer of red material swayed before me. The material had a black border covered in sparkling crystal work. "I want to see you in a sari."

I flopped down into a chair. "Aw hell."

Tahir held up the blouse. It was a skimpy little black thing with a low-cut neck and back. There was crystal work along the bodice. Actually, it was cute, and I'd have no qualms about wearing it with pants or a skirt.

But a sari?

"I bought this for you yesterday," Tahir said. "It goes with your nose ring. And look here." He opened a dresser drawer and pulled out a dark blue velvet pouch. He untied the drawstring and emptied the contents into my lap: gold chandelier earrings, a gold choker, golden bangles, golden anklets, and a gold belly chain.

I was more the antique silver type.

Tahir cupped my face. "Please, for me?"

I sighed. He was seriously asking a lot. If only he weren't so goddamn gorgeous. "I'll do it. But I have a fantasy, too. It's called the maharani and the naughty Brahmin boy."

Tahir kissed me and left the room.

Reaching for the sari blouse, I let the robe slip off my shoulders and pool around my feet.

With the low-cut back and front, a bra was out of the question. Wondering about the jiggling factor, I began doing up the hooks in the front. The blouse was a little tight.

Knowing Tahir, he'd probably picked a smaller size on purpose.

I stepped into the red petticoat and secured it around my waist. The jewelry went on next. Retrieving the small makeup bag from my purse, I lined my eyes with heavy black liner. Might as well go all out.

Finally, I picked up the sari and stared blankly at yards and yards of chiffon.

I had no idea what to do.

Struggling to remember the one occasion I had watched my mom tie on a sari for a dinner party, I tucked one end of the material into the waist of the petticoat, then wrapped the remaining material around me like a sarong. There was supposed to be enough cloth to drape across my chest and cascade down my shoulder.

There wasn't.

I untucked the blasted thing and tried wrapping it again. This was not going well.

Tahir poked his head around the door. "Can I see?"

"This is as close to my going ethnic as you're gonna get," I informed him.

"Then let's take a closer look." Cupping his chin, he walked around me in a circle.

"Well?"

"Definitely better than the fantasy."

He then dropped to his knees in front of me and began arranging the folds of material around my waist.

"What are you doing?"

He pressed his lips to my navel and looked up. "Tying your sari."

This had suddenly turned into my fantasy.

In what seemed like seconds, Tahir had secured the sari around my waist and at my shoulder, creating a perfect fall of red chiffon down my back. I surveyed my reflection in the mirror.

Indian Barbie had met her match.

Tahir came up behind me, wrapped his arms around my waist, and kissed my neck. "You are stunning."

I leaned my head back to give him greater access to my neck. "I know."

His hand slid across my chest and began undoing the hooks of the blouse.

"What are you doing? After all the effort it took to tie it on, you want to take it off?"

His hand slid over my breast. "Well . . . yes."

I closed my eyes. "Just checking."

"Tahir Varun Sahni!"

My eyes flew open to see a massive heaving bosom with a woman attached. I recognized the swarthy features and squat figure from the picture.

Tahir's mother.

My mouth went dry as the most formidable woman I'd ever seen moved menacingly toward me.

Tahir removed his hand and stepped back. "Ma! Your flight wasn't due in until tomorrow!"

I was frozen.

I'd never been this terrified in my life. I went from hot to cold to hot again. My stomach lurched.

Nostrils flaring, eyes shooting sparks, she stood in front of me.

Well, her bosom was in front of me. Her body was actually a few steps back.

Didn't matter.

This wasn't a woman.

This was a dragon.

"Ma, this is Maya," Tahir said.

I opened my mouth to say something, anything.

And puked all over her.

Chapter 47

SUPERMAN HAD X-ray vision.

I had projectile vomiting.

As soon as Tahir had ushered his stunned mother into the bathroom, I'd grabbed my bag and fled in my sari, feeling like an escapee from *The Jungle Book*.

Maybe I was demonstrating a shocking lack of manners, but I didn't think Mrs. Sahni wanted me to stick around. What would I have said to her anyway? "So you're Tahir's mom? Aunt Dimple has said the nicest things about you. Oops, you missed a chunk of upchuck. So you saw your son fondling my breast? Wasn't that funny? Ha. Ha."

So I jetted.

By the time I hit the 73 South, I'd calmed down a bit.

How weird was it for Tahir's mom to show up like that? How the hell did she get in?

Oh right. She huffed and puffed and blew . . .

That was mean. I shouldn't think so negatively about the woman. I loved Tahir. He loved her. So it followed that I should—

Nostrils flaring.

Bosom heaving.

My palms suddenly became sweaty.

Seriously, I hadn't seen anything that terrifying since *The Ring*.

Okay, I needed to concentrate on work—on anything besides Tahir's mother. It was time to form some sort of game plan regarding Sanjay.

I'd cruise home, shower, then conduct a stakeout. Of course I didn't know the first thing about "stakeouting." I was a *Law & Order* fan, but it wasn't like I'd studied each and every episode. Then again, I didn't even know which location to stake out. I highly doubted Sanjay would return to his apartment. What did that leave? Radio Shack? Circuit City?

Or Sanjay's girlfriend, Indira.

There had to be some way to find her. I knew she was a chemical engineer, but that was about it. Ram knew even less.

Speaking of Ram, if he tried to pull me into another meditation session, I'd have to blow him off. Sure, I'd been able to do that cool-white-light-aura-skin-thing stuff, but once again . . .

Pretty much a useless power.

I pulled into my street and stopped, staring in shock. Both sides were lined with cars. I coasted by the house. Our three-car driveway currently had four cars crammed onto it.

Were my parents having a party?

In the middle of a Sunday afternoon?

I was forced to execute a Y-turn and nearly banged into the bumper of a Rolls Royce with a license plate that read: INDIA 1. I knew that car. It belonged to my aunt Renu, the radiologist. She lived in San Jose. What was she doing here?

I finally found a parking spot a few streets down.

Fuming, I walked barefoot up the sidewalk. I'd left my precious Manolos back at Tahir's.

As I approached the house I caught a whiff of incense. By the time I reached the front door I was bathed in a cloud of it.

That should have been my first clue.

In another odd development, stacks and stacks of shoes, bereft of feet, were piled up on the doorstep.

That should have been my second.

I opened the door and nearly tripped over the person sitting right in front of it. He was one of many seated bodies packed into the foyer.

They all looked up at me and stared.

Huh.

Stumbling through the sea of faces, I made it to the entrance of the living room and stopped.

Most of the Mehras had congregated in there. Ram was in the thick of things, presiding over a small fire in the center of the room. My parents were tossing what looked like herbs into the flames. Everyone was chanting. Including the Marshalls from next door.

"*Om kali kali mahakali kalike.*"

Aunt Dimple saw me and let out a shriek. Nadia, seated in the corner looking bored, turned my way and frowned.

Everyone stopped chanting.

Mrs. Marshall grabbed a handful of rose petals and threw them in my direction. Aunt Gayatri nudged her and mouthed the word "later."

Ram threw out his arms. "Jai Ma Kali."

"Jai Ma Kali."

In a rippling motion that started from one end of the room, they all threw themselves forward and touched their foreheads to the ground.

The cat was out of the bag.

At least I was dressed for the part.

Fucking A.

Chapter 48

THE QUICKEST PATH to parental approval?

Be the living incarnation of a goddess on Earth.

It was that simple.

Who knew?

Ten o'clock and the Puja—a ritual in honor of the gods, or in this case, me—was still going strong. Worshippers still filled the house. I was still wearing my vomit-reeking sari, and Ram still presided over the ceremonial fire in the living room.

Speaking of Ram, I had managed to grab one end of his robe as he scooted past on his way to the bathroom. "So you spilled the beans." He gave me a confused look. "Beans, you know, lentils?" Still confused. "Forget it. When did you tell my parents about me?"

"Last night your mummy received a phone call. It seems your cousin Seema is expecting twins."

"She is?" Successful Seema had recently made partner in her law firm. And now she was on the fast track to motherhood.

Ram continued. "I said to your mummy—who cares? So this Seema will be the mother of twins? Bah! Maya is the mother of all creation." He pulled his robe from my grasp and rushed off.

I guess that explained it.

I turned my attention back to the Puja. I supposed it was going well. Any Puja where the house didn't burn down was deemed a successful one.

I had also learned that the rectangular metal receptacle housing the fire was called a kund. It was not a pan for baking brownies as I had previously assumed.

My dad, whom I'd caught dozing off a couple of times, reached over and patted my shoulder. "Very good, Maya . . . very good." He'd said the same thing to me when I'd learned how to ride a bike.

My mom, who was on my other side, kept shooting me smiles, when she wasn't wrinkling her nose.

Well the goddess really needed a shower.

Across the room Mr. Marshall was giving me the thumbs-up sign.

Mrs. Marshall had continued to throw flower petals in my direction at inauspicious moments until Aunt Gayatri had finally taken them away from her. She now sat subdued.

I caught Tahir's eye and he winked. My lips curved in an answering smile. Then I made the mistake of glancing left and making eye contact with his mother. One nostril flared.

Bile rose in my throat.

Tahir and his mother had arrived an hour or so ago. She was wearing fresh clothes and an expression that clearly indicated she was unimpressed by my goddess status. For Tahir's sake, I attempted a weak smile in her direction.

The other nostril flared.

I quickly looked down.

I wondered if anyone had called the press? I hoped not. Even if a call were made, I doubted a reporter would show. They'd liken a Kali Puja in Newport Beach to a Santeria ritual in Placentia. Unless someone performed a human sacrifice, we would not make the front page. Personally, I wouldn't mind a human sacrifice in my honor. I'd even handpick the victim.

Nadia.

She was still looking sulky in her corner. Undoubtedly, she'd tried to leave, but had been prevented by a Mehra. Her secret was safe with me . . . for now.

"Samir will be coming tomorrow," my mom whispered.

I hadn't seen my brother since Thanksgiving. "Oh . . . great."

She smiled, brushed a strand of hair off my forehead, and turned back to the ceremony.

Ram muttered something in Sanskrit, and my mom picked up a metal bowl filled with clarified butter. Using a spoon, she began dribbling it over the flames.

The fire crackled, and everyone resumed chanting.

Aunt Dimple pulled out a pair of small cymbals and began banging them together.

Give me a break!

It was all I could do not to cover my ears and run for my life.

The house was clear.

It was after three in the morning, and I opened all the windows to get the smell of smoke and incense out of the house.

After the Puja ceremony ended, I'd had to sit still and let people come up and touch my feet.

Super creepy.

By the time Mom, Ram, and I climbed up the stairs, I was practically sleepwalking. My dad had sneaked off to bed hours ago.

I opened my bedroom door ready to crash—smelly sari and all—when the sight before me made me gasp.

My room was filled with flowers, gift-wrapped boxes, and tons of cards. I opened one envelope and pulled out three crisp hundred-dollar bills. "What is all this?"

"Baksheesh," Ram said.

My mom explained. "It is customary for worshippers to bring gifts for the deity."

I picked up a dainty blue bag with a familiar logo.

Tiffany & Co.

I could get used to this.

Chapter 49

I LOVED my worshippers.

If I had to pinpoint the exact moment they went from being freaks with foot fetishes to my darling devotees, it would have to be when that nice couple from Dana Point bought me a five-thousand-dollar Segway Human Transporter.

Wasn't that sweet?

I was no longer the unemployed goddess. The perfect career had landed in my lap. Since our house had become a veritable revolving door for the deeply religious, I was totally raking it in. In fact, I was toying with the idea of buying stock in an incense company because of the amount we went through every day.

I discovered that the Puja ceremony I'd walked into on Sunday afternoon was special—to welcome the goddess. Normal Kali Pujas started at midnight and stretched until dawn, which was fine with me. I'm not a morning person.

Basically, for the first two hours Ram would preside over the ceremonial fire and lead the room in chanting.

I would sit on a cushion and try to look intensely spiritual, when in reality, I was thinking up ways to spend all the money people were donating.

Afterward, came the hard part. While Ram continued to stoke the sacred flames, I had to recline on a sofa and hold court while my worshippers approached, offering me a gift in one hand and using the other to touch my feet. Either my mom or one of my aunts would be on hand to take the gift.

Tough. But someone's gotta do it.

It wasn't all reclining on the sofa, drinking wine, and eating chocolate. I had to make sacrifices. I couldn't watch any of my soaps because I slept until two, so I was forced to use TiVo. One of my worshippers had given me a lifetime membership.

I was also forced to wear saris on a regular basis. The black silk one I had on today was shot through with Swarovski crystals. And I had changed my ruby nose ring for a sparkling diamond—naturally I needed my jewelry to match. My mom had spread the word that I preferred silver—and possibly platinum—to gold.

Smoothing the black silk over my knees, I was mulling over the idea of registering at Nordstrom—to make gift giving easier—when Aunt Dimple patted my arm.

"Ah, there's Pinky."

Tahir and his mother were entering the room.

"Pinky?" The dragon's name was Pinky?

Aunt Dimple arranged the cushions behind my back. "Pinky is a common pet name in India."

Tahir approached the sofa. "Maya, I need to talk to you." His voice dropped to a conspiratorial whisper. "It's about Sanjay."

"Later, after everyone has had a chance to meet me."

Tahir looked back to where the long line of worshippers snaked around the room and out the front door. "Can't you take a break? I have some information." His eyes flashed. "And we need to be alone."

I'd barely had any time with Tahir since my house had become the Church of Maya. But I had a career now just as he had his. "I want to be with you, too. Why didn't you come earlier?"

"I was at work until eight. I called, but you were with your hairdresser."

I now had a hairstylist from José Eber come in every evening. It wouldn't do for the goddess not to be well coiffed.

Elegant as usual, Aunt Gayatri, who had come over to switch places with Aunt Dimple, laid a hand on Tahir's arm. "Maya needs to see to her devotees. Why don't you try the halwa?"

Tahir gave me one last look, nodded at Aunt Gayatri, and walked away.

The aunts exchanged places, and it was back to business as usual.

Later, when Aunt Gayatri had gotten up to refresh my glass of wine, I scanned the room for Tahir. I didn't see him, but at the dining table Dimple and Pinky were shoveling halwa into their mouths with fierce concentration. Then I spotted Tahir. He was outside on the deck talking to Nadia.

Hmm.

Aunt Gayatri returned with my drink, and the line of worshippers moved forward.

My aunt was accepting a gift certificate to M.A.C. on my behalf when Nadia sauntered in and perched on the corner of the sofa. Her cheeks were flushed a dark crimson, and I was betting someone didn't know how to hold her liquor.

Inexperienced lushes were so annoying.

"Well, well," she said. "So Goddess Kali waits thousands and thousands of years to resurrect, and when she does, she chooses *you*?" She threw up her hands. "This is one fucked-up Universe we're living in. The human race is doomed."

"Nadia!" Aunt Gayatri admonished.

I smiled at my aunt. "I'll handle this." I swung my legs off the sofa, stood, and adjusted my silver belly chain.

Ram met my gaze and shook his head from side to side.

Was he telling me to show restraint?

As if.

Besides, it was about time I put on a show for my worshippers.

Pure shock and awe.

I closed my eyes and called the Goddess Within. I wanted a little wind, not too much, just enough to give everyone a shiver. The breeze blew through the room, causing a collective gasp.

Then I concentrated until all the lights in the house went off one by one.

The better to see my glowing white aura with.

As the halo of light began to emanate from my body, I could hear the soft cries of surprise. Satisfied that I had everyone's full attention, I allowed the lights to come back on.

Everyone was waiting to see what I would do or say next. I opted for the latter.

I cleared my throat and took advantage of the opportunity. "Just to let you all know, Nadia," I pointed for the benefit of the people who didn't know her, "is not a doctor as she led us all to believe. She is in fact, a nurse. Linda Vista Hospital will verify that."

All the Mehras in the room faced Nadia with identical stunned expressions.

Eyes welling with tears, Nadia lowered her head and fled from the house.

I resumed my position on the sofa, took a sip of my wine, and called out, "Next."

Chapter 50

AS DAWN BROKE through a cotton candy sky, I thought about installing one of those digital counters like at McDonald's. Only mine would say: over one million blessed.

The last worshipper had left, and I was heading up to bed when I saw the front door was still open. I went to close it and spotted Tahir sitting on the doorstep. "You're still here?"

He patted the spot next to him, and I sat down. His eyes were tired and his jaw covered in stubble. "I was waiting for you."

I entwined my arm with his and rested my cheek on his shoulder. "I'm glad."

"You know, I think you went a tad overboard with Nadia. She was humiliated."

So much for snuggling.

I moved away. "She had it coming. What about her crack that I had doomed the human race?"

Tahir reached for my hand. "It's not about her. It's

about you. Have you been out patrolling for malevolence lately?"

I pulled my hand back. "I've been busy, okay? The meet and greet is as much a part of my job as fighting evil."

Tahir gave me a dubious look that roused my ire, and reached inside his pocket, pulling out a slip of paper. "I've been doing some research, asking around. I found her."

"Her?" I took the paper.

Indira Bhatia
GBS Syntex

"GBS Syntex?" I asked. "How did you find this out?"

He grinned. "Through the Indian grapevine. GBS Syntex is in Tustin. I'll take the day off and go with you. We'll just stroll through the lobby, find out where Indira's office is, barge in there, and you can do your cool wind tunnel–mind control thing." He glanced at his watch. "She'll be at work in a couple of hours."

"Well thanks for the info," I said. "But I really need to get some sleep."

"We'll catch her in the evening, then, before she gets off work."

I didn't respond.

"Would you rather go by yourself?" he asked. "I understand. Although I was hoping to see you in action." He smiled and slid his arm around my waist.

"I'll go when I can, Tahir."

His grin disappeared. "What's more important? Sitting around and being petted and pampered, or going after the man who has sworn to kill you?"

I shrugged his arm off me and stood up.

"What's wrong with you?" Tahir demanded.

What *was* wrong with me?

"I just want to enjoy being a goddess for a while. I don't want to think about Sanjay or all the evil in the world. I want to bask in the attention, the love, the smiling faces of my parents and my aunts—who for once—aren't trying to fix my life. I want to be with these people—these strangers—who've come from all over just to see me."

Me.

Maya Mehra.

Gandhi girl.

Tahir slowly rose to his feet. "Maya . . . I didn't realize . . . I'm sorry."

"Yeah, well, you were just trying to help."

He reached out and gently pulled me into his arms. I closed my eyes and pressed myself against him. He kissed me, and we pulled apart. "Now get a good night's, ah, day's sleep, and I'll call you."

I smiled. "Okay."

He smiled back and turned to walk down the drive.

Without thinking I blurted out, "Can you tell your mom to maybe ease up on me a little?"

Tahir stopped, shoulders rigid. "What did you say about Ma?"

Oops.

There was no going back now. "What I mean is, I threw up on her, and that was bad. But I apologized, didn't I? So why does she glare at me like she's a sleeping cobra and I'm the little boy who's been poking her with a stick?"

Well it was a good metaphor.

Tahir slowly turned around. "She's come to every one of your Pujas, hasn't she? Have you ever taken the time to talk to her?"

"Talk to her? I can barely get within ten feet of her. She's drenched herself in Eau de You're Not Good Enough For My Son."

Tahir took a step forward. "Listen, the reason Ma flew in was because I told her how serious I am about you. I want her to get to know you, like you . . ."

"Why do you even care what your mom thinks? We love each other. That should be enough."

Tahir's laugh was abrasive. "Well it's not. That's the difference between India and America. I care what my parents think. I need for them to approve of the woman I love. I need their blessing. Couldn't you try—"

"Try what? Try to be a different person? Your mom obviously wants a typical Indian daughter-in-law who quietly pours tea and doesn't speak her mind. I'm American. Screw that. I'm a goddess."

Tahir looked at me for a long moment, then turned and walked away.

I tossed my hair. Whatever. I needed my beauty sleep.

Tomorrow night my worshippers would be waiting. I turned to go back inside when—

"Maya?"

My brother Samir was coming up the walkway. He was on the shorter side—like all Mehra men—and had always been quiet and serious. I noticed he'd ditched the glasses, grown his hair, and had a leather satchel slung across his chest. He looked good. Stanford seemed to be agreeing with him.

"Hey," he said.

"Hey."

He shoved his hands in his pockets. "So you're really a goddess."

"Yeah."

"Cool."

"Can be."

"Well, I drove all night, so I'd better get some sleep."

"Me too."

Together we entered the house.

It was the longest conversation Samir and I had had in years.

Chapter 51

TAHIR WAS just being a bitch.

He'd come around.

The little voice inside me, covered in dirt, crawled up from the hole and tried to say something. I clubbed her over the head for good measure and pushed her back in with my foot.

I was never one to subscribe to that sacrifice-everything-for-your-family Indian shit. Unfortunately I'd fallen in love with a guy who did.

What I didn't get was why Pinky was so opposed to my relationship with her son? She and Aunt Dimple had made the match in the first place. It couldn't just be because of the vomiting.

I had a sudden sneaking suspicion.

Picking up the cordless by my bedside, I dialed Aunt Dimple. "Tell me more about your lunch at McDonald's with Pinky," I said by way of greeting.

My aunt was eating and talking at the same time, and her reply was unintelligible.

"Aunt Dimple, can you not eat for a few minutes please?"

"But I'm hungry," she cried. "All morning I have been running around buying candles and incense and sandalwood—your mother has me doing all the hard work—I only had time for toast and egg in the morning. And then a Cinnabun and chocolate milk shake at the shopping mall."

"I'm sorry. But I need to know if Pinky really agreed to my match with Tahir."

Aunt Dimple was silent.

I rubbed my forehead. "I won't get mad."

"Well," my aunt said slowly, "she liked your picture. She thought you were very pretty. She was happy you lived with your parents and not on your own doing God knows what. The age factor was appropriate—I had lied about that, you see, because you look so young—"

"It's okay," I assured her. "Go on."

"But she wanted a girl born and raised in India, with Indian values."

"I knew it!" I couldn't keep the triumph from my voice. "I knew you lied!"

"I did not lie," Aunt Dimple protested. "I wanted the two of you to meet because I knew it would be love at first sight. And it was, no?"

Not.

She continued. "I spoke to Tahir. I told him he had to meet my niece Maya."

"Told or begged?" I asked.

More silence.

I closed my eyes. "Forget it. What's done is done. I just wanted to clear things up."

"But Maya, you're a goddess! It is most auspicious to have a goddess in the family. Pinky will surely see that. Better than having a daughter-in-law who can cook and organize the household."

"Good-bye." I hung up.

I sat back against the pillows. So that explained it. Aunt Dimple had fudged the facts. Tahir's mother had never approved of me in the first place. She'd probably told Tahir to at least meet me just to make my family happy, and he'd agreed because we were providing him with room and board.

None of that mattered now. I had no intention of trying to win Pinky over. It was an impossible task anyway. Tahir had to choose. His mother or me.

I had a sick feeling I already knew the outcome.

I wanted to wallow in my thoughts. I wanted to burrow under the blankets. I wanted to be alone.

My bedroom door banged open, and Ram rushed in.

I shrieked and pulled the sheet up to my chin. I was wearing a thin white cotton tank top that skimmed my ass, and no bra.

"Rise and shine," Ram said happily.

"This is highly inappropriate," I snapped.

He waved his hand. "Bah. Every day the beautiful ebony statue of Kali-ma is undressed and bathed in milk by the chosen priests of our temple. At night she is dressed again."

"I'm not a statue, Ram!"

"That is true."

"What do you want?"

He sat on the edge of the bed. "I have found a most worthwhile organization. They rehabilitate snakes that were mistreated or abandoned as pets and release them into nature. You and I shall pay them a visit this afternoon."

"Snakes? Snakes give me the creeps—anything with scales does." Including Tahir's mother.

Ram wagged his finger at me. "Snakes are good luck. They are worshipped in India."

"I thought snakes were considered an omen," I argued.

"Some worship snakes, some fear snakes, it is essentially the same thing," Ram countered.

It might have been the afternoon, but it was still too early for me to try and make sense of what he just said.

"I'm not going, Ram."

He wagged his finger even harder. "A goddess must take care of her children. She must give back to the community. Half of what you are given must in turn be bestowed on those who need it."

"Fifty percent!" I sat up and the sheet dropped to my waist. Ram's eyes widened, and I quickly lifted it up again. "You want me to give half my money away? Christians only give ten percent! I need this money, Ram, and I'm not giving it away. Especially not to a couple of snakes! I'm buying a condo." I folded my arms and stared at him stubbornly.

Ram sighed and sat up. "I cannot force my will on yours. I will go alone. There is much you still have to learn, and it is clear I will not be the one to teach you. I have failed."

"Come on, Ram—" I began, but he had already left.

I got out of bed. Ram had left the bedroom door open, and I went to close it when a burly red-faced man in overalls walked down the hallway. "Can someone tell me where to set up the new altar?" He looked at me, and his eyes bulged.

"Oh, grow up," I snarled, and slammed the door in his face.

Chapter 52

BY DINNERTIME Ram still had not returned.

My mom nervously tore her chapatti to shreds. "What should we do? Why didn't I give him my cell phone?"

I got up from the table. "I'm sure he's fine." It was time for me to start getting ready. First, a long soak in a tub filled with milk, almond oil, and rose hips.

My dad pushed back his chair and burped. "Maya's right. After all, if something had happened to Ram, she would have sensed it."

Umm.

This wasn't the time to inform my parents as to the extent of my powers. I'd spent enough years being a disappointment as a daughter. I didn't want them seeing me as a disappointment as a goddess.

My dad was scooping out a bowl of vanilla ice cream and my mom was heaping more food onto my brother's plate. In an Indian household the son is forbidden to have an empty plate. Samir rubbed his stomach and looked faintly ill.

No one was looking at me, so I turned around and quickly called the Goddess Within.

I tried to zero in on Ram like I'd done with my parents. I didn't feel anything.

Huh.

Well as long as the feeling wasn't bad, that was good, right?

I went up to take my bath.

I stepped out of the tub, tying the towel around me when my mom ran into the bathroom.

Seriously, did anybody ever knock around here?

Then I noticed her pale face and the phone pressed to her chest. "What's wrong?"

"There was a call," she gasped. "An accident."

I could feel the coldness seeping into my chest. "Ram?"

She nodded. "He's at the hospital."

Chapter 53

I DIDN'T GO to the hospital.

I made the excuse about needing to stick around in case any worshippers showed up.

The truth was I couldn't face Ram.

I should have gone with him to that stupid snake farm or wherever the hell he went. I should have protected him.

I could just imagine the conversation my parents and brother were having in the car. "Why didn't Maya *see* this? Why didn't she prevent this?"

What was the point of going to the hospital anyway? It wasn't like I could heal him.

I flopped down onto the couch and buried my face in my hands. I knew who was behind Ram's "accident." I should have annihilated him when I had the chance.

Ugh.

The malevolence hit me at the same time the phone rang.

It was Sanjay.

If he was calling collect, I'd vanquish him.

I ran to the kitchen and grabbed the phone in midring. "Sanjay, you bastard, what'd you do to Ram?"

"How does it feel, when you can't even protect the people around you?" he questioned smugly.

Rage boiled up inside me. "He's an old man. And he's your cousin!"

"He's a damn nuisance," Sanjay spat. "He was always criticizing my apartment."

"I will find you."

Sanjay laughed. "I overestimated you this whole time. Now everyone will know what a joke you are." He laughed again.

"Are you going for that whole maniacal laugh thing? 'Cause your voice is far too nasal to pull it off," I pointed out.

"You'll never find me," he said coldly, and hung up.

I quickly punched star sixty-nine. The automated voice informed me that although the service was working . . . blah blah blah.

I stood there, closed my eyes, and tried to zero in on Sanjay. I strained so hard I nearly burst a blood vessel in my brain.

Nothing.

When the doorbell rang I ignored it—I knew it was an

early devotee—and went upstairs to my room. I retrieved the slip of paper Tahir had given me.

Indira Bhatia
GBS Syntex

Maybe there was still a chance to redeem myself. I only hoped it wasn't too late.

Chapter 54

BY 7:00 A.M. I was in the car and headed toward GBS Syntex in Tustin.

Well, technically, I stopped off at Starbucks for a vanilla latte first, and then had to wait in a long line with a bunch of morning commuters.

So by seven-thirty I was on my way to Tustin.

I'd gotten the directions off MapQuest, and the tall glass building was hard to miss. I parked and noticed that half the cars had Cal Tech bumper stickers. I passed through the entrance and skirted a group of nerds to get to the circular reception desk. "Can you tell me where Indira Bhatia's office is?"

The young woman frowned. "Ms. Bhatia no longer works here."

The news hit me like a blow. I felt faint. "Are you sure?"

"She quit."

"When?" I whispered.

"Yesterday was her last day."

I reached for one last straw. "Do you have a number where I can reach her? An address? Do you know if she started another job? Please, I'll take anything you can give me."

Her frown deepened. "I'm not allowed to divulge such information, but it doesn't matter because I don't know. She wiped all her personal information from the computer database, which really messed up the system. Now I'm going to get stuck after work uploading all the new stuff and—"

I turned away. The hope within me died.

There was no point trying the Goddess Gaze, the receptionist was telling the truth.

If only I hadn't waited. If only I'd listened to Tahir.

But not about his mother.

Navigating through a cloud of failure, I trudged back to my car.

Nadia was right. The human race was doomed.

All because of me.

Chapter 55

I SAT ON my favorite stretch of beach.

Thank God it was winter. I couldn't imagine wallowing in misery with chattering children building sand castles nearby and horny teens rubbing suntan oil on each other.

I had decided to give up my dharma.

I wasn't going to do the goddess thing anymore.

I'd get a normal job like normal people and stop off at Starbucks at a normal hour and develop normal ulcers and die with all the normal regrets.

Kali could be reborn as someone else next time.

My worshippers would have to find someone else to idolize.

Of course my Malevolent Meter would still go off, but I'd have to learn to ignore it. In the beginning it would be hard, but if that guy in *A Beautiful Mind* could turn his back on all the voices in his head, then I could turn my back on malevolence.

Maybe it wasn't the right or moral thing to do.

But it was right for me.

Before I knew it I was crying.

Tahir had never called. I had thought he would. He and Nadia were probably consoling themselves together, both of them running down my list of faults, with Tahir's mother jumping in every time they forgot something.

I'd been so close. I had Tahir. I had Ram. I had a house filled with people who adored me. I had money and gifts. Nadia was the family leper. In short, my life for one happy moment had been perfect.

A perfect sham.

My parents were proud of me, for what? I hadn't accomplished anything. They were proud of me for something I had no control over. Like being proud of a child because he or she has beautiful red hair or amazingly green eyes.

Where was the value in that?

I hadn't even tried to take Ram seriously. If someone else had been in my place, she would have unlocked her full potential. She would have become the Goddess Within, instead of having to call her up all the time. Now Ram was lying in the hospital.

And what about Tahir? I'd insulted his mother to his face. Sure, Pinky made Endora on *Bewitched* look like the ideal mother-in-law, but Tahir loved her. I should have respected that.

Tahir was better off without me.

Had there even been anything "real" between us? All we had was sex.

Really good sex.

Unbelievable sex.

I mean the orgasms were just . . .

Anyway.

With regard to my poor worshippers, what had I done for them? I hadn't listened to any of their problems. I hadn't eased the burden of living or anything.

And I'd turned my back on the snakes in need.

Sanjay was right. I was a joke.

A celestially spoiled brat.

I lay back on the sand and closed my eyes. I was going to lie here until the tide came in and swept me away. Suicide was the answer.

Good-bye.

A seagull flew by and crapped on my face.

My eyes flew open, and I looked down at my watch. Barely an hour had passed.

I sat up and gazed at the ocean. Either I'd have to move closer to the water, or I'd have to scrap the suicide plan and go home.

I stood and headed back to my car.

Across the street was a small park with a playground and picnic tables. Three of the tables were overflowing with Hare Krishna Hippie Freaks. Their orange robes reminded me of Ram.

Ram . . .

I could feel the tears building up again.

A few of the Hare Krishna men were crossing the

street and heading toward the beach. One of them stopped and smiled at me. "The Universe doesn't make mistakes," he said.

"What?"

"Think of all the planning it took just so you and I could smile at each other in the middle of the street."

"I'm not smiling."

Smiling even wider, he cocked his head. "Did you know that you have bird sh—"

"Yes," I said curtly.

"Okay then." He waved. "Have a blessed day."

I watched him walk away.

The Universe does not make mistakes.

Huh.

And then it hit me.

Just like that.

No bells. No whistles. No eons spent under a tree communing with nature. Just instant clarity.

The Universe in all its infinite wisdom had chosen me. The same Universe that created the Pacific Ocean, and redwood forests, and puppies with oversized paws, and kids with gap-toothed smiles and vodka and Johnny Depp.

And me.

I wasn't a failure. I was divine.

I'd been given this dharma. I'd been chosen for a reason.

The Universe does not make mistakes.

Maybe someone else could do the job better.

Tough shit.

I'm the one the Universe chose.

And then I did something I'd been too afraid to do before. I called the Goddess Within. Pulled out my compact.

And looked in the mirror.

Nothing scary. Just me.

Covered in bird shit.

But me all the same.

Chapter 56

HOAG HOSPITAL was a state-of-the-art facility located off the 55 freeway and Pacific Coast Highway. The doctors there liked to surf, then shop at the Nike Town down the street.

That was Newport Beach for you.

I washed the crap off my face in the ladies' room, then went to the reception desk.

"Last name?" The nurse asked.

"Last name?" I was baffled. Ram was just Ram. Thankfully I saw my brother inserting coins into a coffee machine and raced off. "How's Ram?" I asked him breathlessly.

He blinked at me from behind his glasses. "Ram? Oh he's fine. Minor concussion. Did you know Hoag has eighteen LDR suites? I checked out their ambulatory surgery floor. I haven't decided on a specialty yet, but obstetrics—"

I tried another tactic. "Where's Ram?"

He blinked again.

"Samir?"

"Sorry. I was just wondering if I could check out the imaging center. Ram's in Room 407. Mom and Dad got him a private suite."

I took off.

Ram was propped up in bed looking cross while a nurse poked and prodded him. He shot her an offended look. "Please do not handle my person in such a manner. The body is a sacred vessel for the soul."

The nurse snorted. "Right. Ask me how many sacred bedpans I've changed today."

Catching sight of me, Ram's frown disappeared. "Maya!"

"I'll be back later," the nurse said.

Ram stuck his tongue out at her retreating back. "Bah! Irritating woman."

I reached over and hugged him. "I'm so sorry I didn't come earlier. I'm sorry about everything."

Ram cupped my face in his hands and stared intently into my eyes. "You have done it. You and the goddess are one."

I sat in the chair closest to the bed. "I finally realized that I had to stop trying to be the goddess. I am the goddess. Does that make sense?"

Ram sighed happily. "Yes." After a moment his brow furrowed. "Perhaps it was a language problem that kept me from explaining this to you?"

"We both speak English."

He waved his hand in dismissal. "You do not speak

proper English. Half the time I cannot understand what you are saying."

I rolled my eyes. "Like, whatever."

"About Sanjay," Ram began.

I leaned forward. "I will get him. But first I want to know what happened. How did you get hurt?"

For some reason Ram looked embarrassed. "I was petting a cobra when Sanjay entered the building. I was alone, having been given free rein to visit with the snakes."

I repressed a shudder.

"Sanjay began waving a gun, telling me I must go with him. Luckily, I noticed the nervous glances he kept darting at the snakes. He is very scared of them, you see. Silently, I communicated with my cobra friend, and she hissed in agreement. As Sanjay approached, the cobra coiled and struck at his face. Sanjay screamed, dropped his weapon, and ran out of the building."

"Wait." I gave him a puzzled look. "Did you say you communicated with a cobra?"

"Snakes are very intelligent creatures."

"But I've never seen you do anything incredible like that."

"Why then did the cobra attack Sanjay and not me?" Ram questioned defensively.

I dropped the subject. "How'd you get the concussion then?"

The embarrassed expression was back.

"The lift was taking too much time, so I chose the

stairs. Some naughty child had left a sticky sweet on one of the steps. My sandal became stuck, and I tripped over my robes and fell down."

"Oh." So Sanjay hadn't hurt Ram? If he'd stuck around outside, though, he would have seen the paramedics arrive. Naturally he figured fate had stepped in and done the deed for him.

Sanjay was such a loser.

I took Ram's hand in both of mine. "I'm going to go, okay? I think it's time Sanjay came out of hiding."

Ram smiled. "I always believed in you."

"Earlier you said I was practically unteachable."

"Bah! I had a concussion. I was rambling."

"You didn't have a concussion then, Ram," I pointed out.

His expression grew stubborn. "I never doubted you for a moment."

I squeezed his hand. "I couldn't have done it without you. You are the coolest Brahmin priest I have ever met."

As I got up, Ram said, "One day books will be written about you."

I tossed my hair. "Yeah, and I can just see the reviews. *Prozac Nation* meets *A Passage to India*."

And then, once again, I was running out the door.

I nearly ran into Samir in the hallway.

"Hey, Maya, you want half my Snickers?"

Did he really need to ask? "Thanks." I popped the

chocolate in my mouth. "Have you been here all morning?"

He yawned. "It can get lonely in the hospital. Mom and Dad are at work, and I thought, Ram should at least have someone to talk to."

I smiled. "You're going to make a kick-ass doctor, you know that?"

Samir blinked. "Thanks."

I suddenly realized why my brother and I had never gotten along—it was simple—there was no reason. I had mistakenly assumed that because we were different, we would have nothing to talk about, no way to relate. "Listen," I said, "before you go back to Stanford, maybe we could go out for drinks or something? Catch up?"

He blinked twice. "Okay. That'd be fun."

My little brother and I. Spending time together.

He was right.

It would be fun.

Chapter 57

EXITING THE HOSPITAL, I nearly ran into someone else.

Note to self: Running with my head down is dangerous and does not add to speed.

I looked up and into a pair of deep black eyes. The kind of eyes that could make a girl swoon.

If she were so inclined.

"Hi," Tahir said.

"Hi." Okay and my next line? "Umm, are you here to see Ram?"

"Actually, I was looking for you. Your cell phone was off, and I tried the house. Took a chance you might be here . . . how's Ram?"

Ram? Who the hell cared about Ram at a time like this? "You were looking for me?" Threads of hope encircled my heart and made it pound.

"Maya—" Tahir stopped as a very pregnant woman and her harried-looking husband brushed by us.

"Don't," I said before he could finish his sentence. I

couldn't let him go on. Not when I'd been in the wrong as well. "Don't apologize."

He looked puzzled. "Apologize? I didn't come here to apologize."

Now I was the one looking puzzled. "You didn't?"

"What is there to apologize for?"

Huh.

"Why are you here then? Aren't you supposed to be at work?"

Tahir neatly stepped aside as a teenage boy on crutches came hobbling by. "I was supposed to take Ma to Universal Studios and took the day off."

"What happened?"

"I decided to see you instead. She'll deal . . . as they say."

I laid my hand against his cheek. "The three of us will go to Universal Studios together."

Tahir covered my hand with his and kissed me.

There we were in the hospital parking lot. I wasn't one for PDAs—public displays of affection—but after a few moments in Tahir's arms, I forgot there had ever been bird turd on my face.

"Wait." I pulled away. "We have issues. We can't just kiss and make up."

He pulled me back. "Of course we can, hence the expression."

My mind was spinning. A few hours ago I was ready to sleep with the fishes. But things had changed. I had changed. "Tahir . . . I'm the goddess. I really am."

"To me you always were." And then he added almost as an afterthought, "I think we should get married."

"Okay, I may be a goddess, but I'm also messy, extravagant, and I sleep ten hours a day."

His lips brushed my forehead. "I'll do the cooking."

"Thank God." I wrapped my arms around his waist and laid my head on his shoulder.

He nuzzled my hair. "You take care of the world, Maya. I'll take care of you."

I closed my eyes. "It's a deal."

Chapter 58

USING MY DIVINE navigation system, I tracked Sanjay down to a suburb in Santa Ana.

Amazing the things you can do when you believe in yourself.

Gag.

Regardless of how After School Special it sounded though, the fact was, as soon as I truly believed I would find Sanjay, I was able to close my eyes and locate him.

Well almost.

I wasn't able to get an exact address, but I knew I was close.

I roamed one street after another until I struck gold.

Tucked between a beauty salon and a Dairy Queen was a shop called India Emporium.

Hmm, an Indian market.

I'd found gossip central.

The interior of the shop was cool and dark and heavy with the scent of spices.

Since I had cleverly deduced that Sanjay was staying with Indira, I also cleverly deduced that Indira would have to rent her Bollywood DVDs and buy her masalas and Indian staples somewhere.

The middle-aged clerk behind the counter wore a gray polyester shirt and black pants. "Excuse me, do you know someone by the name of Indira Bhatia?"

Before he could answer a high-pitched female voice piped up from behind a shelf of Indian pickles. "Mandira or Indira?"

"Indira," I said.

A tiny woman with black hair down to her waist stepped into the aisle and faced me. "Indira Bhatia on Hillcrest Drive or Indira Bhatia on Maple?"

"Wait, there's two of them?" I asked.

"What DVDs does she rent?" the man behind the counter asked. "The Indira on Maple likes the oldie goldies but Indira on Hillcrest likes the new releases."

"Chee, you are such a dumbo!" the woman exclaimed. "Don't listen to my husband. Describe your Indira to me."

"Her hair is scraped back into a tight bun, and she wears glasses. She's a chemical engineer."

"That is Indira on Maple only," she said, and her voice dropped to a whisper. "But she is no longer having a job."

"That's definitely her."

"She was in here with a young man."

My voice dropped to a whisper as well. "He's her boyfriend. They're living together."

Her eyes widened in shock.

"And that's not all," I added. "This same boyfriend nearly murdered a pundit. You wouldn't happen to have Indira's address, would you?"

"Yeah, yeah," she said. "Dumbo will give you the address."

The next moment she was practically running into the back room. Before the door closed I saw her reaching for the phone.

Grist for the gossip mill.

The husband handed me the slip of paper with Indira's address on it.

"Thanks, Dumbo," I said automatically. "I mean, ah, thanks."

And then I was—what else—running out the door.

I stood in front of a nondescript small yellow house. Sword in hand, I was the Goddess Within.

Remember. Try stealth.

I hesitated, then thought what the hell and kicked the door down.

Stealth was boring.

I stepped into Indira's front hall. "Come out, come out, wherever you are."

Sanjay and Indira really should have known better.

They'd never stood a chance.

Chapter 59

SANJAY CAME DOWN the stairs with, of course, a gun. Indira clung to him from behind.

Seriously, though, as soon as I took out Sanjay, I was going after his gun supplier.

Sanjay was not engaging in the proper use of firearms.

I stood there with my hands on my hips. "You know, Indira, you really picked a winner. Thanks to him, you've lost your job and your reputation."

"Reputation?" she asked.

"I told the people at India Emporium that you and Sanjay were living together."

"You mean the Shahs from India Emporium?" she shrieked. "But they'll tell the Gulatis, who will tell the Ambanis, who will tell the Ramanis and Aruna Ramani's parents live in the flat next door to my parents!" She pushed Sanjay away and sat down on the bottom step. "They'll kill me."

Sanjay kept the gun trained on me but looked pleadingly at Indira. "Don't worry, Indu."

"Oh shut up! My life is ruined."

"What is it you see in him anyway?" I asked. Sanjay glared at me.

Indira cupped her face in her hands. "I like that he has goals, dreams. Otherwise, computer programmers are a dime a dozen."

"Goals like destroying me and Bill Gates?"

She shrugged. "Makes him interesting."

Sanjay switched the gun from one hand to the other.

That got my attention. I was the goddess, not a relationship counselor.

"You will never succeed," he said.

"Why the gun then?" I argued. "If you're so sure I'll fail?"

For a moment he looked dumbfounded.

"Because it is my dharma to kill you," he finally said.

"Are you sure that's what your dharma is, Sanjay?"

"Yes," he insisted.

That was the problem with fanatics. They were so damn sure about everything.

I took a step forward. "Then we have a slight problem. Because I'm sure about my dharma. I know without a doubt that I'm here to save the world. I still have a lot to learn. I'm far from enlightened. But I'm never going to give up. And no one is going to stop me. So you see the conflict of interest here? You've sworn to stop me, and I refuse to be stopped."

"She's right, Sanjay," Indira called out.

"But Indu," he protested.

"I'm bored with this," she said. "I want to do something different. All you ever do is sit around and plan how to destroy Maya. I want to go to Vegas."

"Indu . . ."

They continued arguing, but I was no longer paying attention. There was this curious roaring in my ears, like the flapping of thousands of wings. The warmth inside me fired up into something intense, something scalding.

I saw myself riding bareback though a sunset valley on a beautiful black stallion. In one hand I held my sword, in the other a decapitated man's head.

The man was Sanjay.

I didn't know what the vision meant, but I did know one thing.

I was so feeling the shakti.

I'd have to ask Ram about the weird vision. What was up with the horseback riding? I'd never been on a horse in my life.

The familiar wind started up, without my being aware of having called it.

"It ends here, Sanjay."

He looked at me, and whatever he saw made him open his mouth and step back.

Without any effort I pried the gun from his hands. With just a thought, I increased the wind's intensity so Sanjay was flung back against the hall closet door. Indira was hanging on to the banister for dear life. The wind had loosened her bun, and her locks spun around her face.

I thought the wind-tousled look really did it for her.

"You have a choice, Sanjay. You can live, or you can die. If you live, it will be by my rules."

He stared up at me without answering.

I prodded him with the edge of my sword. "The Goddess of Destruction does not ask twice."

"Live," he whispered. "I'll live."

I kept the sword trained on him but silently ordered the wind to disappear.

It did.

Yes!

Okay, so I was being a little dramatic with the wind and giving Sanjay the choice between life and death, but it wasn't like I could send him to jail. On what charges? It was my word against his.

And I didn't really want to kill him. "Rise," I demanded.

Sanjay did, and I looked him straight in the eye. "You will leave California. You will move to Seattle and pursue your dream of destroying Bill Gates. Your desire to create a software program to rival Windows is a worthwhile one. Focus on it. I never want to see you again. If you come near me or mine again, I will know. Believe me, I will know."

I could see in his eyes that he understood. Maybe it was my whole new well-adjusted Goddess of Destruction persona, maybe it was his desire to keep Indira happy, or maybe I had just succeeded in transferring his fanaticism from me to Bill Gates.

Whatever.

Indira threw herself to the ground at my feet. "Jai Ma Kali!"

I cocked an eyebrow at Sanjay.

He followed suit. "Jai Ma Kali!"

How I loved my worshippers.

Chapter 60

I WAS ON A ROLL, so I decided to cover one last base.

Linda Vista Hospital.

Not as nice as Hoag, but I wasn't there for the ambiance.

She was sitting alone in the cafeteria, nursing a cup of coffee.

Nursing, get it? She was a nurse . . .

I took a seat across from her. "Hey, Nadia."

Her hair was limp and her T-Zone dripped with oil. I didn't mention any of it though.

"What do you want?"

I tugged on my lower lip with my teeth. This was going to be painful. Better to do it fast. "I'm sorry. What I did the other night was uncalled for. You didn't deserve that."

I was wrong. Fast didn't mean painless.

Her eyes narrowed with suspicion. "Why are you apologizing?"

She didn't believe me. And Ram thought I had issues!

"Nadia, I mean it. I had no right to treat you like that. I'm really sorry."

She folded her arms and sat back. "Give me a break. You are so full of it."

This wasn't working. I'd have to use the Goddess Gaze.

Before I could do so, a doctor with a bandana covering his curly brown hair sauntered over. "Could I interest either one of you ladies in a breast exam?"

Nadia curled her lip. "Not even if you were George Clooney in the second season of *ER*."

"Not even if this were some sort of parallel universe and a pathetic remark like that was actually a turn-on," I said.

He moved away with a dazed look, and Nadia turned to me with a grin.

"Listen," I said. "Do you like your job?"

"I love it," she said without hesitation. "And I'm damn good at what I do."

"I believe that."

"I guess, in a way, I'm glad everyone knows the truth. I hated pretending."

"Tell me about it."

"I don't think you'll suck as a goddess."

I smiled. "Thanks."

She smiled back. "Anytime."

Chapter 61

"THE BANNER is crooked," Ram said.

"I've adjusted it three times," Tahir said, taking a sip of his scotch and soda. "I'll be damned if I do it again."

It had been four weeks since I'd converted Sanjay and Indira, and I hadn't heard a whisper from them since.

We were throwing Ram a bon voyage party at the house.

I put my arm around him. "Relax, Ram, and finish your Coke."

He took a sip and made a face. "Bah! Someone has put lemon in it. I will exchange it."

Before he could walk away, I grabbed the sleeve of his robe. "Have you thought more about the vision I had, Ram? The one with the stallion and the decapitated head?"

He rubbed his chin. "Were you sleeping?"

"I was wide-awake. I told you."

"It means nothing."

"But—"

"The children are drinking all the Coke. I must go now." He tugged his robe away and hurried off.

Sometimes I wondered about Ram's priorities. I shook my head and concentrated on my dirty vodka martini.

Pinky joined us. "It is a nice party, Maya," she said. "You have done a good job."

"Thank you," I said with surprise.

"You know," she added, "it is fine to enjoy a drink now and then, but it should not become a habit. It is different for men, of course. They work hard all day and come home and want to relax."

I was about to respond when I caught Tahir's eye. I choked back my retort and smiled. "You're right."

Well it wasn't like I had to live with her.

She smiled back. "Have I told you any stories about when Tahir was a baby? He was absolutely perfect."

Tahir laughed. "Ma."

Pinky reached over and affectionately smoothed the collar of his jacket. "He never fussed as a child. All you had to do was place him in front of a mirror, and he would happily look at his reflection all day. It was his favorite pastime."

Tahir's smile disappeared. "Ma."

I excused myself as a new party guest arrived. "Nadia, I'm glad you made it."

"I brought someone. His name's Doug, and he's a cardiac surgeon. He's parking the car."

"Great. Can't wait to meet him."

She ran her fingers through her hair. "So you and Tahir really are getting engaged."

"Yeah."

She smirked. "I give it three months."

I tossed my hair. "Does Doug know those aren't your real boobs? 'Cause you might want to tell him that in reality, his thirteen-year-old nephew probably has better cleavage."

"Bitch!"

"Skank!"

We took off in opposite directions.

Thank God things were back to normal.

My brother walked over with my drink and handed it to me. "Thought you might need this."

"Thanks."

"You should come up to Stanford," he said. "I could show you the campus, we could go into Frisco . . ."

"I'd love that."

He blinked, smiled, and walked away.

Mom, Aunt Dimple, and Aunt Gayatri were supervising the buffet table. I joined them.

"I took the check down to the shelters, Maya," my mom said. "Half to the homeless shelter and half to the animal shelter like you requested."

I was helping out our furry four-legged friends at the local no-kill shelter. Maybe I'd eventually reach out to snakes.

I was suddenly struck with a terrible thought. "You didn't give away my Segway, did you?"

My mom rolled her eyes.

She was doing that a lot lately.

"You only reminded me ten times," she said.

"Thanks," I said, and hugged her. This time she hugged me back.

"Can I ride the Segway, Maya?" Aunt Dimple asked, her mouth full as usual.

I put my arm around her and squeezed. "No."

Aunt Gayatri was surveying Tahir. "What's his sperm count? Have you checked? If they're sluggish, come to me right away."

Ram and Tahir were waving me over, and I was grateful to get away.

"So." Ram beamed. "When will you be coming to India?"

Tahir slipped an arm around my waist. "Soon."

I looked at him. "Actually, my answer was never."

"But you should come before the wedding," Ram said.

"Wedding?" What were they talking about? "We haven't planned anything."

"I'm thinking a Delhi wedding," Tahir mused. "I've asked Ram to officiate. Do you know we met before? I didn't realize it until now, but Ram and I were on the same flight to LAX." Tahir's eyes narrowed. "Were you the one who burned a stick of incense in the lav?"

So that's why Ram and Sanjay jumped me at LAX. I was wondering why they'd chosen such a public place. I cleared my throat. "Back to this wedding business—I was thinking more Dana Point and not Delhi. We can book the Ritz."

"I was meditating," Ram explained.

"You can't go burning incense on a plane," Tahir pointed out. "It's dangerous and against regulations."

"Where is it written?" Ram argued.

Ugh.

Malevolence was on the move.

It was getting to the point where I didn't have to be in close contact. A fifteen-mile radius was my limit.

But I was getting better every day.

Ugh.

"I have to go." I brushed past them, mentally checking that my sword was in the car.

"Maya," Tahir said, catching up to me.

"It's going to be like this," I said. "Malevolence doesn't care about convenience."

Tahir leaned over and kissed me. "Go. I'll save you a piece of cake."

"Two pieces."

Ram waved. "See you in India!"

We were really going to have to talk about that.

And then I was running out the door.

AVON TRADE...because every great bag deserves a great book!

Paperback $10.95
($16.95 Can.)
ISBN 0-06-053079-0

Paperback $13.95
($21.95 Can.)
ISBN 0-06-059036-X

Paperback $13.95
($21.95 Can.)
ISBN 0-06-056143-2

Paperback $10.95
ISBN 0-06-059562-0

Paperback $13.95 ($21.95 Can.)
ISBN 0-06-056337-0

Paperback $10.95
ISBN 0-06-052227-5

Don't miss the next book by your favorite author.
Sign up for AuthorTracker by visiting *www.AuthorTracker.com*.

Available wherever books are sold, or call 1-800-331-3761 to order.